W9-CHS-385

Rear View Mirror

by

Vanessa Leigh Hoffman

To Abby,
Best Wishes—
Vanessa J. Hoffman

DORRANCE PUBLISHING CO., INC.
PITTSBURGH, PENNSYLVANIA 15222

This is a work of fiction. Names, characters, places, and incidents are either the product of the author's imagination or are used fictitiously, and any resemblance to actual persons, living or dead; events; or locales is entirely coincidental.

All Rights Reserved
Copyright © 2008 by Vanessa Leigh Hoffman
No part of this book may be reproduced or transmitted in any form or by any means, electronic or mechanical, including photocopying, recording, or by any information storage and retrieval system without permission in writing from the publisher.

ISBN: 978-0-8059-7730-1
Library of Congress Control Number: 2007943397

Printed in the United States of America

First Printing

For more information or to order additional books, please contact:
Dorrance Publishing Co., Inc.
701 Smithfield Street
Third Floor
Pittsburgh, Pennsylvania 15222
U.S.A.
1-800-788-7654
www.dorrancebookstore.com

To a special friend
I told you I would do it
And I did it.
May you rest in peace.

Prologue

"I love you!" She wanted to scream that phrase over and over again throughout her neighborhood that night, but she didn't. She knew she had to free up her mind so she could start writing in her journal about a heart-wrenching seven-month drama involving two semi-sweet love affairs that should have taken off to new heights. As she looked out her bedroom window at the star-filled sky, she wondered why they weren't allowed to. She had to come to grips with the strange turn of events in this final chapter of her life. Sitting in her candlelit room, dressing, watching her new husband pace up and down the front yard walkway, she suddenly knew her future wouldn't be allowed to evolve into anything, due to fate...greed...and deception.

Introduction

It started one warmish March day on a St. Petersburg bayside, at an open-air bar named Captain Al's Waterfront Grill and Bar. She had been laid off her so-called permanent teaching position at a rather snobby naval academy for elementary and middle school students. Her young students had been surprisingly down to earth; she didn't know how that was possible. So she decided that when the clock struck two fifty-five, she was out of there. Why stick around? She had given the best she had during the past two years, and they snubbed her, took her for granted. She was ready for a drink, some sun and fun, and relaxation, and that was straight where she headed—to Captain Al's.

She slipped into a lawn chair as soon as she arrived and started gazing at the boats and at the skyline of her newfound city on the bay. She had moved here from Canada a year and a half ago, and it was still heaven to her. She felt exuberant, just sitting there, until she got a taste for a cold beer. She walked up to the bar. Nonchalantly, she sat down on a stool next to an empty one and noticed there were cigarettes still on the bar.

Next thing she knew, an older man was sitting right next to her. They started talking. Vibes were there. This man was older, still attractive—so much so that anyone could tell he used to be a looker, a real looker.

He was a distinguished grey-haired gentleman of medium height, very well-groomed, with a hint of expensive cologne on his well-manicured and postured frame. He walked very elegantly to his stool.

He asked her name, and she his, and they immediately broke into a conversation about their lives. He said, "Call me Kenneth." He was magic to her. It turns out there was a twenty-six year age difference between them. She was forty-two. He was sixty-eight. Something attracted them to each other. It was like a need each of them had in which both of them satisfied the other. The course was now set. They were destined to meet the next day at the same bar, same time.

Along with the other daily bay cronies who frequented the bar, there were a few newtimers to the scene. Johnnie, who lived downtown and worked at the Veteran's Hospital as an electrician, and Kat, or Spider—either name applied. The latter rode a ten-foot tall tricycle which he used for transportation, as well as for a sales model. He was selling his invention for only eight hundred dollars. That was a pretty steep price in her estimation for a novelty item like this contraption. There was one intellectual-looking, dark-haired young lady who wore black horn-rimmed glasses and tucked her silky hair behind her multiply pierced ears. She always sat at the table right beside her, reading some avant grade book, whenever Kenneth was late. On one of these occasions, Natalie, as she introduced herself, asked to join her. The intellectual dramatically expounded on her addiction to crystal amphetamines, her obsession with the green peace movement, and her insatiable desire to fuck the long-haired, blonde, and tan tricycle inventor. She was never so glad to see Kenneth's face coming towards her than that day. She never sat near the intellectual's table again.

There were tons of tourists who flocked this bar daily. Some were dipsy and good, others cunning and bad, and yes, the other thirty-three percent were comprised of weirdoes and lunatics. These were the types Kenneth told her he encountered every day as he sat and stared, casting a line out into the bay. This was his recreation. Kenneth never killed a fish. He only did this as a sport. Once he snagged a line, he removed the catch and sent it back to live in the warring sea. You see, he was just too kind-hearted to kill anything, even an insect. It seemed he possessed everything needed for happiness in life—sportsman, socializer, rancher.... What?...Rancher? Yes!

She was definitely impressed on this first day of introduction. He proclaimed that he had a ranch near Sarasota, in a small livestock and citrus town called Parrish. It was a big ranch, five thousand acres of prime orange-growing and cattle-producing land, stretching from near Ellenton to the Skyway Bridge. Kenny had a white picket fence circling around his massive property and told her to come on out if she got a chance. He said, "It's easy to spot. Call me, and I'll come out to the gate." Kenneth continually expounded on his enormous house, with its wrap-around porch and balcony and its lush amenities. He noted that his house was dressed up all in white, with green shutters. Kenneth equated it to a Georgian plantation house, back in the day. He was supposed to have many workers living on the land in their own houses, as well as his niece, Jude. Jude was the veterinarian on site, as well as his stability, he said. Gimpie was the manager of the ranch who came in every morning promptly at seven A.M., and was the only one who did not live on the ranch. She lived in Ellenton with her new husband, and they rented an apartment. Now Jude, on the other hand, was flirtatious, spontaneous, and, when mixing with her best friend, Kimmie, an outstanding jockey on the West Coast, they became every man's worst nightmare. Jude lived on the ranch and had an office and bungalow in Pinellas Park. She was in California about every weekend, flying herself on her uncle's Lear jet. Yes, Kenneth said he also had a sharp, cool Boeing sitting in the backyard of the ranch house, waiting to take off with her in it at any moment.

As she began to leave the bar, after her third draft, he asked her to sit for a few more minutes, because he had to tell her... something very important...something she might not believe. He told her of his military duties in Korea, Vietnam, Kuwait, Afghanistan, and Iraq. "Being a two-star general leaves one with no time to ever be at home," he said. That was why, he said, he had retired to Florida when he reached the early age of fifty-five, sacking a net worth of five hundred and twenty-five million dollars, four hundred and seventy-five of this net being liquid.

She didn't even flinch. It was at that point that she realized money and status were not what was keeping her hooked on the man; instead, it was the time, place, and circumstance.

She met Kenneth there every day, promptly at three-thirty, and they drank beer until six. He would then walk her to her car and take off himself, not in a fancy auto, but rather on foot, with fishing pole and tackle box in hands. He was definitely an eccentric spirit, and she treasured him from the start. He said that he owned an apartment building downtown, near the pier, and he kept the front living space for himself when drinking at Captain Al's. They began to call each other several times a day, just to chat and laugh. They were really beginning to enjoy each other's company. He was so fun, smart, and witty, and he had a really cool Boston accent. Some of his words sent tingles down her spine, and the fact that he was a two-star general, who now owned a ranch located thirty minutes away from her house, didn't hurt matters at all.

Chapter One

As I sat on the edge of my bed, looking out the window and feeling uneasy with all that I was looking at, I wondered if I had truly erred. I thought about that life-changing early March afternoon, and I scribbled some words on a page with quivering penmanship. I was lucky enough to have a few empty moments, and so I let my mind drift back to the beginning, to the start of the amazing cycle of events that had taken place over these past months.

As I wrote, I heard the sounds of the swirling winds blowing through the rough waves, causing crashes on the sea wall of the St. Petersburg pier. My small red convertible was racing down the lane, ready for a valet-parking attendant to ask for its keys. It was a warm day, plenty of sun for all of the fishermen who were straddled out on their Florida Gator lawn chairs, just waiting for a short, taut pull on their long, sagging lines.

I strolled past these sportsmen, who couldn't keep their eyes on the water. I looked at my watch, noticed it was three sharp. *Yes*, I thought, *time for a cold one*. I sat at a sunny bar table, ordered a beer, then soon noticed an empty stool in the cool shade. And so I sat solo, next to the sunglasses and cigs sitting by themselves on the bar.

After five minutes, an older gentleman returned to occupy his empty seat, not knowing that his and my life were about to change, and I mean forever. So we chatted and laughed, sometimes even hysterically. Kenneth, as I soon found out he was called, didn't even dream of what they had in store for him at this point. He found out a little too late.

The next day, Kenneth returned at three sharp, as he said he would. I stayed at the bar for only an hour. Kenneth bought beers for the patrons and told war stories. He had fought in the Korean, Vietnam, and Gulf Wars. In the Gulf War, he sliced Khomeni's cheek. In the Vietnam War, he had been a prisoner of war and had his teeth knocked out by a shovel at the hands of his Hanoian captors. At the beginning of his air force career, Kenneth was transported to Korea to act as an air-traffic controller at the U.S. base at Seoul. He was shot with shrapnel pieces throughout his body during the first week out. He was immediately flown to Boston, his hometown, for treatment, then discharged with a purple heart. This was sounding more and more like a B-rated movie to me, but I let it go.

Kenneth was a staunch Democrat, which I thought to be a little odd due to his strict military beliefs. His only wife, Jane, had been a strident Republican Party member until her rather early death at fifty.

Jane and Kenneth had only been married for two and a half years when Kenneth told Jane to pack up and move back with her parents. There was a fifteen-year age difference between them. He constantly referred to Jane as his child—he'd never had any. One day after returning from Colorado Springs, where he had been speaking at a war memorial event, he walked into his house and down the hall into his brown-leathered wall study and found Jane's parents mulling around his personal paperwork, which was piled up on his desk. They were nosing through bills, pay stubs, and banking receipts. He immediately ordered everyone out of his house, called his lawyer, and a divorce was set in motion. He never stopped loving Jane, however, only her family. He thought he was just too much of a free-spirit for her.

For instance, one night when Kenneth was in his twenties, he and his air force buddy stumbled into a local sushi bar. Very drunk already, they ordered two more each. The establishment declined to serve them any more at that point, so Kenneth proceeded to kick the huge fish aquarium, spilling water and goldfish throughout, ruining the restaurant's newly installed plush carpeting. The police were called, but Kenneth and his buddy, "Rock," were gone—gone to the next bar, where they were apprehended by authorities and taken to the city lock-up. Luckily Rock's uncle was a state prosecutor and got both boys released with no bail, no pending court appearance.

Ten years later, when Kenneth took Jane out to a dinner on their two-year anniversary, he took her to the same Nagasaki Kitchen in Boston. There was no more fish tank, however, and it appeared more elegant and expensive. As the couple strolled through the entrance, the proprietor shot one glance at Kenneth, then escorted him out the door. He pushed Kenneth to the exit and said, "You're not welcome here, and don't come back."

Jane was furious with Kenneth and very embarrassed. She asked him what he had done to cause this, and he told her the truth with the usual "I'm sorry" puppy dog look on his face. This episode, coupled with others like it when Kenneth would leave her alone in movie theatres, shopping malls, and churches so he could go drinking at the nearest bar, caused her to become very disgruntled with her marriage. This inspired Jane's parents to look through his papers to see how much money he really had. You see, Kenneth spent so much money on his own extracurricular entertainment. Everyone thought Jane deserved more respect as she was the backbone of the marriage. Up to this point, Jane had threatened to leave him three times, so when Kenneth walked out on her, she—and everyone else—was devastated.

Chapter Two

We had been meeting at Captain Al's every day for over six months at the same time, except for on weekends when we met at noon. We made more and more friends—patrons, bartenders, and managers of the establishment. One day, however, Captain Al's was closed due to flooding from a near-miss hurricane, and so we went upstairs to the top floor. We found an open-air place called Xanadu. There, he told me of his massive wealth and that he had acquired this solely through raising angus beef and Florida oranges. He did have a little stock on the side.

My expression never changed, even as he raved on and on about his Lear jet and Kimmie's escapades. Kimmie was like his adopted daughter. She was the actual daughter of one of his servicemen friends who lived in Salem, Massachusetts. His friend and his friend's wife had been flying to Bali for a long-awaited twenty-fifth wedding anniversary celebration trip when their jet voyage took a turn for the worse. The airplane went through an incredible amount of turbulence from a massive rainstorm, then plummeted downward on its side. It was lost on the radar screen, found only the next morning by a fisherman who had strayed off course from the shore of his native homeland of Borneo. He reported seeing an incredible amount of different-sized shiny metallic shapes floating on top of the water. Crews searched the wreckage of what was found to be Kimmie's parents' doomed flight but found no survivors.

Being Kimmie's godfather, Francis had been given the responsibility of raising her if anything ever happened to the parents. She moved in with him at the ranch, went to a brand-new private academy and proceeded to become a narcotic-filled recluse.

At the age of seventeen, right before her high school graduation, she was given a horse which she rode daily, for hours at a time, at an incredibly fast speed. She had taken plenty of jumping lessons as a child but enjoyed the sensation of racing more. She fell in love with her thoroughbred stallion, Marty.

Marty became faster than lightening as they galloped through the ranch fields in back every morning and evening, partly due to Kimmie's expertise with horse obedience and health issues, but mostly because of his golden genes. At nineteen she signed up for her first derby. It was a small-town race in Georgia, where she placed a reputable third. Kimmie knew what she now wanted from life, to become a famous female jockey. She was off to a good start with her talent, her horse, and most of all, her godfather's money.

Kenneth invited me to fly out to Los Angeles to see Kimmie's race at Hollywood Downs. He said I could stay in my own room at the Beverly Hills Hotel, sip on champagne by the pool, and eat dinner nightly at the Brown Derby. I took him up on his invite for some time in the near future. I advised him I was scheduled to take a trip up to my birthplace of Quebec City next week for a two-week stay. There I was to help in a massive carport sale my mother was scheduled to have. She was seriously contemplating moving down to my area of St. Pete.

Kenneth asked me how I was able to keep up car and house payments with no job. I said it was very tough at present. I had a little bit of savings and the hope of getting a phone call from a stern-sounding principal offering me more money than I had before in my contract. It never happened...well...it hadn't happened yet, but I told him I wasn't giving up hope. Kenneth told me he had a plan to get my former position back...if I wanted it. He had served with the one-star general who was offered the position of getting the slacker teenage boys disciplined or thrown-out at my former academy. This general supposedly would do anything Kenneth asked of him, so if I wanted my job back, I could get it back.

* * *

Boarding the plane for Quebec City, I had a strange feeling of urgency to get the job done there so that I could hear more of Kenneth's life. After three hours, I landed in Quebec. Baggage in hand, I hailed a cab for my mother's home. She lived in one of the more exclusive areas of the city, close to fancy shops and elite churches and schools. She wanted less of a strain in her life however, as her bills and property taxes were soaring. So we started the selling of some of her more prized possessions, along with some of her lesser ones. After three days, the huge sale was over. There had been cars and people lined up and down the driveway and street, waiting for the doors to open, as if in a much publicized estate sale. The next evening was when I got the call from Kenneth. He said that he was flying his jet to Fort Bragg, North Carolina, the day after tomorrow, to commemorate a war hero who died in action during the last days of the Gulf War. He was asked to come at the widow's request. He told me he could swing by the airport in Montreal to pick me up, maybe go out to dinner, and then continue onward.

He wanted me to be his dressed-up lady to the hilt at this military funeral. He informed me this would take place in four days, and he told me to bring something cool to change into after the ceremony as it was extremely hot and muggy in North Carolina in June. I agreed and went to sleep, dreaming of castles, maidens, and knights in shining armor sitting in my doorway waiting for me—for whatever fate had in store for me.

* * *

Camille Bisset's fairytale dream state was about to be ruined by the incessantly loud ring of what seemed to be an alarm clock, or telephone. It was the latter, as there was no clock in her room. She got out from underneath her smooth, clean sheets, quickly put on her long, flannel robe, which she wore on spring, fall and winter nights in Quebec, and groggily answered it, the receiver stationed at her ear. When she heard Kenneth's gloomy voice she perked up right away. She stood at attention...what was the matter? Was there some problem? And why was he calling at five-thirty in the morning?

Kenneth told her he was feeling lousy, had been up all night, and had seen the doctor earlier that day. He said the intern ordered him not to fly any type of aircraft feeling like he was. The malady seemed to be, perhaps, a type of walking pneumonia. The doctor wasn't sure without further tests. Obviously they weren't going anywhere...not to North Carolina and not to Hollywood Downs, not anytime soon at least. Ohhhh—how fate wheels and deals.

Chapter Three

I came home to St. Petersburg two days later with a little bit of spunk and enthusiasm—couldn't wait to call Kenneth and see if he was all right. Nobody answered his phone but a machine; I left a short message of "Hello, just checking on you. Call me later." I got a return call not more than four hours later at two o'clock in the afternoon. The voice, however, sounded different, a bit more anxious—not as subdued as I was accustomed to from his character.

When I finally talked to him in person, he quickly asked me to meet him at Fresco's Waterfront Bistro at the marina, where "the prices are right and the martinis are sizzlin'." When I had entered the restaurant in the past, he walked up to escort me to the table, and he always said that phrase to me...not today, however.

I saw Kenneth from afar, waiting for me, sipping a Heineken, contemplating life. He arose from the table as soon as he saw me and greeted me with "Hey, Zahz." Kenneth loved using nicknames for people instead of their "boring given names," as he always said. When he found out that I used to call myself "Zahz" when I was young, he started calling me "Zahz." He loved the name, and it stuck. He extended his arms to embrace me, but not in his usual fashion of hugging me while rubbing my back. I thought to myself, *Oh well.* Then he pulled out my chair, sat back down, and ordered another brew.

He said to me, "I have news to tell you. I am really a four-star general, still over command troops in Iraq." He said he felt too boastful to brag anymore of his accomplishments, so he just left it with everybody as, "Yes, I'm a two-star general who only supervises in this capacity from time to time." But yes, yes, he was so much more than just that. He was strong, tough, and my hero, and he said he wanted to live with me at my house until the ranch was ready for another tenant, the other tenant being me. He said that it would probably be for only a month.

I quickly said, "Sure...just help me with the mortgage and you're golden."

He added, "Soon I will have my two boys come to your house to do some light remodeling and finish out the garage apartment, then we'll sell the place." Right now, it had on itself an array of code violations from its previous owner, of which I had to take the burden.

"Never worry. All things work out. Good always comes to those who wait patiently and faithfully," my grandmother used to say when my brother and I stayed with her in Nova Scotia and looked in the huge toy shop windows at Christmas time. We loved our grammy. She basically raised us. We spent all our summers and most of the winters with her. Our mother and father divorced when I was three and Bradley was one. It was hard for mother to make ends meet when we were little until she got a pretty good job in management at a top clothing store in Quebec City. We didn't know much about our father, other than he died five years later from a heart attack while digging out land to lay some railroad tracks. He only gave my mother money from time to time and when we weren't around. Coming home early from school one day, I looked in the front window and saw my father holding cash in his hand. He was cornering my broke and desperate mother in the kitchen. She cried. He then picked her up and carried her to the couch in the den, where he raped her. I heard *ma mere* screaming. My father and mother never knew that I saw and heard this, and I never told them I did. This was the only time I saw my dad. I didn't know who was at fault in their marriage. My mother never spoke of the divorce—or my father, for that matter.

Struggling to get out of the heavy, pensive mood I had laid upon myself, I added, struggling, "Ya know, I would love to have some company on my ranch." I had a fairly big front yard for a St. Petersburg, Florida, home, very shady, with gardens on either side...my paradise, for now.

The next day I picked up Kenneth in the front yard of his city apartment. He was holding three tool boxes, an electric saw, and a fishing pole. He proceeded to climb into my small red convertible, and we journeyed to my tiny home in the center of the city. My house was three miles from the bay and three miles from the gulf in both southward and westward directions. The breeze felt at the location I inhabited felt so invigorating, especially during a potential hurricane. Hurricanes in Florida seemed to be fortune-filled for builders and building supply manufacturers, but only an out-of-control, paranoid joke to the seasoned, veteran inhabitants of life on this flirtatious mid-Floridian gulf coast.

We went to my house, unloaded everything, and Kenneth proceeded to organize the work on the completion of my garage apartment. He was like a work horse. He had so many years on him, but so much spirit and strength left. I loved him even more for helping me with this project and was even more looking forward to moving into his kingdom on the hill in Parrish, on Tampa Bay, where fairy tales were to turn into reality... hopefully.

Chapter Four

A few days after moving in with me, Kenneth was called back to the ranch for a week's worth of duties that consisted of breaking in wild horses just bought by Emilio, and for a very cheap price. I called him and asked him, "Kenneth, when do you think I'll be moving into the big house?"

He replied, "When you think you're ready."

What did that mean? I wondered, and so I continued to wait.

He told me he was to schedule his two ranch "fixer-uppers" to come to my garage apartment to redo its violations. They never showed up...not for three days. Finally one afternoon, after talking to a very serious Kenneth—who was filled with excuses—about this issue, my obnoxious but harmless next-door neighbor and I decided to journey to the heavens and back to Earth, by way of the Skyway Bridge connecting Pinellas to Manatee counties across Tampa Bay. After five or ten more minutes of interstate, I saw the exit Kenneth was always saying was the route to get to his place. Every day at the bar he asked its drinkers to come visit him at the ranch, never thinking any one of them would. That was not the case. I had to finally get a glimpse of the estate's grounds.

Bobby and I continued a short while on Kenneth's route until we came upon the massive white cross-barred fence, constantly being mentioned by Kenneth. He was very proud of this feat. He referred to this as his greatest accomplishment to date as he had fenced the entire three thousand acre ranch himself, with the occasional help of the two laborers. I sped up to the ornate gates on which was spelled out THE RANCH in cursive type. Here I found a nonchalant, evasive Kenneth who never even invited me through the gates and onto the grounds. He just waved, turned, and walked away.

I was dumbfounded. Bobby said, "See, I told you he would turn out to be a jerk—and bi-polar, besides. You know you've only known him for seven months."

I put my Cabrio in reverse and got the hell out of there. We drove back to our respective residences in silence.

I waited all evening and night for a phone call from the man I thought I loved and who loved me, but to no avail. I waited two more days, and still, nothing.

* * *

Almost one week before, Francis had been surveying the grounds of the ranch, watching Kenneth when he was on property. He knew he had to drug Kenneth over a period of time, so he plotted. He sneaked into the manor home late one night and replaced the codeine pills, which were given to Kenneth on a regular basis from the Veteran's Administration hospital, with mild, slow-acting arsenic. Now Francis prioritized confiscating Kenneth's infamous clientele book, duplicate keys to the black ranch Escalade and silver Lear jet, and, most importantly, all of his checking account withdrawal and deposit information. It was now time to set out on his long planned mission.

* * *

It was a cool Halloween night, and the vampires and gargoyles were cheering as Francis silently strolled inside the massive manor home. He knew exactly where to go; he had done this once before when he had replaced Kenneth's baby aspirin with low-dose arsenic tablets. He had ordered architectural home layout renderings from the county code compliance department in downtown Bradenton immediately after his first meeting with Camille at Fresco's, two weeks prior. Both times he entered the mansion he wore black leather boots with gripping rubber soles, and he went up the stairs and down the hallway. The floor never creaked. These boots he thought to be the perfect device for a smooth entrance and speedy exit, and they evidently were.

He nudged the door, which was already ajar, until it was fully open. He entered into the cozy, professionally-decorated, maroon-walled bedroom and sitting lounge. This was where he found an Escalade key chain on the nightstand with both a car and Lear jet starter, a thick clientele book, and a checkbook, all on the coffee table in front of the sofa. He gathered up all these crucial items, then glanced across the room. He was aghast looking at the man with the uncanny resemblance to himself stretched out on the mattress. Francis felt like he was looking into a mirror. He couldn't believe his eyes. In his almost seventy years of living, he had never seen two people who looked more alike.

Francis knelt, head in hands, weeping—not for the deed he was about to commit, but for a life he had never even been given a chance to acquire. In this sullen state of emotion, he abruptly fell into unconsciousness.

Chapter Five

When Emily walked into the unwed mother's shelter looking for a hot meal and warmth, she was greeted by an array of peddler's trying to sell their wares of adoptive families. She had never even entertained the thought of selling her baby. As Emily appeared to be a young, pretty, healthy girl in her middle teens, she was approached by all kinds of wheelers and dealers. Each had photos of their prospective families and homes, along with income verifications. Amounts of money were offered by each dealer. Her head was spinning, and she felt like she was sinning even talking with these people, who resembled players in one of her father's many all-night poker games. Emily took a long, deep sigh and stated to each party, "I'm much too sleepy to make a huge decision like this tonight." They offered to come back to the shelter in the morning. She said, "Fine. Just don't have me waked-up if I'm still sleepin'."

Uprooted from a dairy farm near New Hampshire, five-year-old Emily and her brother, three, moved to a tenement structure in Boston because of lack of funds due to "Artie," her father, who had a gambling addiction. Artie had put his farm and dairy cows up as a bet in a poker game. He lost. The new owners now lived in luxury, due to the prosperous business they had inherited, and Artie and his family now lived below poverty-level standards. Artie kept saying to his family, as he always had, "Don't worry. This will soon pass. The gods are just testing our strength."

Well, it never passed, and the family lived there until Artie's death six years later, which was soon followed by his wife dying of a broken heart. Artie had been sick with emphysema as he smoked two to three packs of cigarettes per day. It finally got the best of him. His immunities simply wore out.

Emily and her brother were tossed from one family to another, like juggler's balls thrown from hand to hand in a side show, staying two months here, half a year there. One day, however, Emily was tossed alone to a rather opulent foster home. Emily never heard from her brother again. She adored her new family and felt like Mr. and Mrs. Jehl were her real parents. She went to a high-society private school, made good grades, and went to dances, followed by dates, with eligible young men.

On one of these dates, however, she found herself in a compromising position in the back of a pick-up truck. She and her date were parked in a hay field close to the academy she attended. Emily knew only the young man's name and where he went to school—nothing more.

At sixteen, when even a day late for a period, intense fear and doom hovers over any girl. Needless to say, in the 1930s, when a young girl of sixteen was seen with a protruding belly, it raised many an eyebrow. Emily couldn't bear telling her foster parents the sordid truth, so she left home. She skipped town, hitching rides along the way, until she arrived back in Boston. It was the only place she really felt comfortable.

She stayed in homeless shelters for the first three nights and days, until she was told to check out the unwed mothers' shelter. "There," Emily heard, "they take care of everything." So Emily went there one evening, only trying to seek refuge, and never left alive. A rich Manhattan couple, the Redmans, who had recently moved to Holsbrook, offered her "dealer" a very good sum for her baby, which she took. She felt there was no other way out. She had no home and no money to raise the baby. The baby's father never claimed responsibility; doing that would have ruined all of his chances for getting a law scholarship at Harvard.

When she finally went into labor at the shelter, she gave birth to twins. From the start she had a high fever, which never cooled down even for one second. She simply went numb, then gave up on life. Emily died, leaving her twins' lives, placing them each in powerful, feuding grips, one in the hands of God, the other in the hands of the devil.

The dealer felt very fortunate upon hearing about the twins. He thought that perhaps he might make another few thousand from the second baby. After the babies were cleaned, checked for health problems, and left to sleep for hours, they were then given to Emily's "dealer." Of course, now that Emily had died, there was no monetary distribution. It all went to the broker.

The first baby was a boy, with blonde fuzz and freckles. The second was a boy baby as well, with blonde fuzz and freckles. He was identical to the first, except for the massive red birthmark under his left eye. The broker did not want anything to do with this "mistake baby," as he referred to it, nor did any other broker. The shelter was forced to release this "mistake baby" to the area orphanage. In the black market world of baby buying in the 1930s, everything had to be in line; otherwise. there was no sale.

The perfect boy baby was carefully placed in the hands of his newfound inheritance. The three of them stumbled to their coach, carrying bags of jewels and feathers. They proceeded to gallop onward toward the pulley drive that acted as a bridge over the moat to their castle.

It was the perfect life for any toddler to have, with numerous friends, parties, games, pets, and, most importantly, toys.

The "mistake baby," or Francis, as the orphanage decided to name him, grew up not having the perfect life. He never saw an animal, only during one hour-long visit to the Boston Zoo. He never experienced a toy, a game, or a party in his first few years of childhood. Fate had really dealt Francis a bad blow from the start. In primary school he made failing grades. In junior high he made passing grades, and in secondary school he made honor roll. Francis began to feel a glimmer of hope, but he was still fighting one major obstacle...poverty.

At eighteen, Francis left the orphanage and went to work for a small landscaping company outside of Boston proper. This lead had been given to him by one of the administrators at the orphanage, along with a recommendation. He made a fair living—not enough, however, to pay rent on an area apartment. He answered an ad in the Boston globe under "roommate wanted." When the advertiser answered his phone, Francis asked how much rent was per week, and "Only ten dollars" was the short response given. Francis thought this to be a fair price, so he agreed to meet with the occupant to complete the deal. The next morning Francis took the train from the shed where he was bunking on the landscaping company grounds, where the owners were nice enough to let him stay until he found shelter somewhere else. This local train took Francis into Boston, near Beacon Hill. This was where he found the apartment's address.

He stumbled up to the door, knocked, then heard a loud, brisk, "Who's there?" Francis answered the voice. The screaming reply was, "Well, get the hell up here."

Francis carefully walked up the rotted planks of wood on a staircase that had no railing, until he reached the top, where there was only one apartment door. The tenant stuck his filthy head outside of it, stared at Francis blankly, and yelled, "Well, don't just stand there staring at me. Put your body through this opening and *entrée*." He attempted to speak his last sarcastic utterance using a French accent, but instead he came off sounding like an East Coast redneck. Then the man bowed, showing Francis the makeshift path of entry. Francis had to squeeze between dusty objects and dirty clothing rags to get to a closet-sized back room where the tenant was pointing to a card table with a stack of messy papers on it. The landlord said assuredly, with arms folded, "This is the place." The small room smelled like mildew and had a wet, clammy feeling; however, Francis had little choice. He had no where else to go. This was the fork in the road that finally made him realize he needed to work in some other line that he might be able to live a decent, normal life.

He had acquired a small savings that could get him through almost a month, and with this in mind he turned in his notice at the landscaping firm. They wished him luck, and he hit the pavement in search of money. This quest proved more difficult than he had ever imagined. "We're not hiring," "You have no qualifications;" "Don't think so, young man," "No experience?" were a few of the remarks made to Francis on a daily basis. He soon went from being a jovial, hopeful, and somewhat irresponsible young man to a cynical, callused, and serious, worn soul from this experience.

One evening, at the end of his month-long job search deadline, craving trivial conversation and lots of libation, he moseyed into an Irish pub near Fannial Hall and ordered three Guinnesses and one corned beef and cabbage. The smell made him remember those Friday nights at the orphanage when corned beef and cabbage with new potatoes was served religiously. It was one of the few treats that the orphanage provided its "inmates." They looked forward to this meal all week long. The cook was from Ireland and just worked two days and two nights per week, as that was all the orphanage could afford. During the other five days, leftovers from these four meals, and canned and jarred foods were served. Francis had become great friends with this cook, Mr. O'Sullivan. Mr. O'Sullivan even let Francis cook the meals with him from time to time. Francis never forgot Mr. O'Sullivan's recipes and his knack for knowing the correct measurements of spices and other ingredients needed for flavor without ever using any measuring device, just gut feelings. Since Francis Cranford, the surname posted on his birth certificate, was supposedly of Irish descent; he was very interested in learning more about his culture. He really loved picking up a British Isles geography book or an

Irish cookbook. Francis used to tell Mr. O'Sullivan the made-up story given to him by the orphanage. He would drone on and on about how his parents came over on a ship from Ireland to Boston, where they both acquired malaria during a horridly hot summer. They soon perished, leaving he and his twin brother to be placed in separate city orphanages. Again and again he thought about his lifelong desire of meeting his twin, and he always asked himself, "I wonder if he's getting through life all right? I wonder where he is right now?"

As the meal was placed in front of Francis, he thought the aroma scintillating. He eyed the first piece of cut meat, savoring the thought of that scrumptious bite of juiced-up corned beef, and he placed it in his mouth. "This is no good!" he shouted as he began to chew. "Not real"— not the way it's supposed to be, ya hear?"

The cook came over to Francis' corner table and asked him, "What's the matter with it, fellow?" Francis knocked the plate off the table and demanded that he, himself, go to the kitchen and prepare the dish "the way it's supposed to be."

After serving up several Irish dishes later that night to more than satisfied clientele, Francis was immediately offered the cooking job at the pub, which he grabbed. He was to make more money now, so he would be able to move into a small one-room apartment by himself, the thought of which he treasured. Everything was going great now, both personally and professionally.

* * *

Getting everything he asked for "at a moment's notice," Kenneth Redman became a crashing bore, filled with temper tantrums which seethed out at any given moment. He became very hard to live with in elementary school and junior high. He was simply a smart, conniving young man who wanted everything for himself. He decided he liked the act of taking much better than the act of giving. He felt destined for the thriving, successful business of pulling the wool over other's eyes. As a teen, he began to make a lot of money, becoming a master con artist. It came easily for him. He had watched his father do it for years.

In his senior year of high school, Kenneth held every heart in the class. He had girls waiting in line for a chance to date him and be seen with him.

Kenneth had a huge ego and did not even want to waste time with "mere mortal activities, like sports," he would always tell his cohorts. He chuckled to his classmates during one lunch period, "I'm going straight to the top just on my charm and wit." He was soon offered two scholarships, a partial one at Yale and a full one at Florida Southern University, in Lakeland. He chose the second offer, as he had enjoyed vacationing in Sarasota, Florida, at the family's gulf front bungalow when he was a youngster. He absolutely adored the horse industry there, so much so that Kenneth went out of his way to become a expert horseman in every sense. This became his number one hobby.

After a two-year stint at Florida Southern, he decided college was not for him. He felt like living the entrepreneur-life of his father. He had become a clone of his foster father, Thomas Redman. He began work outside of school in the banking business in Miami. Then he switched to selling stocks, bonds, and mutual funds. He learned how to double, even triple, an allotted sum of money and what investments most generally provide for this type of yield. After a few years, however, he felt he had hit a brick wall. There was no more room for his intense desire of growth, both in egocentrism and wealth. There was nothing more to learn about making scads of money that the financial news wouldn't provide. He was at the end of his rope, and he became very bored. Hating to leave Florida, he felt he had to return to Holsbrook, where he was raised, and move in with his parents...at least for a bit. They finally convinced him what to do next.

Kenneth did whatever his hero advised him to do, without any question. Listening to his humble father's teachings always ended in success for Kenneth, so he took Thomas at his word. Thomas said, "Enlist in the military. It will toughen you up, bring you down to earth, and you'll realize your vulnerability. It's hard, but you'll grow to love it." He was right. Kenneth became a great war hero in both aspects, fighting and commanding.

Chapter Six

Kenneth's visit to Holsbrook, Massachusetts, turned into fourteen years of tumult. He enlisted in the air force when he first arrived in Holsbrook and was quickly flown to Seoul, Korea, to act as an air traffic controller. This happened to coincide with a crucial air strike in this 1950s war. Kenneth originally dreamed of becoming a fighter pilot, but instead the air force thought his highly strategic mind to be an important tool in getting U.S. planes safely on and off the ground.

Late at night, during his first week of duty, he was trafficking solo. Suddenly a Korean plane flew straight over the tower, almost hitting its roof and blowing shrapnel pieces around the bright, star-filled sky, almost like confetti being thrown at a party. Kenneth collapsed on the board.

The next thing he knew, he was looking out a window at a dreary, snow-filled sky. He asked a lady standing before him dressed in a white smock, "Where am I, and what happened?"

She smiled and answered, "You're in a military hospital in Boston. The air force flew you back home after you were hit with shrapnel in Seoul. You seem to be doing swell now."

Kenneth asked, "When can I leave?"

The nurse replied, "Give it a few days anyway. Do you have to be somewhere?"

Kenneth chuckled and said, "Always."

Kenneth was discharged three days later. He had bumps all over his body from the pieces that were lodged in his flesh; however, the doctors said the lodged shrapnel would pose no threat in later life. Kenneth received a Purple Heart for his heroism and begged to be sent over once again to complete his mission. The air force agreed after more recuperation. This time Kenneth served for one year as a fighter pilot, then he was elevated to the rank of lieutenant.

When the next Asian war broke out in the sixties, which we joined later, Kenneth was sent. After two years of intense fighting in the sky, he was promoted to captain. One afternoon, while on assignment near Hanoi, his helicopter was hit by fire. It spiraled downward, one hundred feet to the ground.

Luckily the copter had just taken off so there was no fire upon impact. The Vietcongs took over the helicopter and its soldiers. Kenneth and his boys were taken to a small, dirty thatched hut with no furniture to speak of, just a sturdy palm leaf that was glued with sticky tree sap onto three small pieces of wood. This was where the enemy commanding officer sat while assessing the situation.

This hut contained six American prisoners of war. They each slept in their own space of slightly dug-out dirt. Kenneth showed his soldiers how to do this with their hands, remembering what his two German shepherds, Belmont and Mattie, would do in the heat of summer by the Gulf to keep cool. They would dig down deep, and once they got low enough, close to the water that ran beneath the sand, they felt comfortable. This was the only remedy for surviving the "jungle hot mug" in Vietnam, as the soldiers would call it.

The captors only fed the prisoners one small meal per day, and most often it consisted of one tiny piece of fish from the pond out back; some unusually textured, weird tasting peas bought cheap from the vendors that strolled by; and a piece of unripe fruit picked from a tree alongside the hut. Sometimes it was simply a bowl of tasteless sticky rice. The six months the emaciated prisoners lived there seemed like an eternity.

One night Private Wilson asked Private McCree, "Hey, do you want to flee this joint? Today I found an opening in the wire fence about five hundred yards away. We could squeak through, then get back-up to get the others out. Maybe we could get some kind of recognition or medal, or something."

Private McCree said, "Count me in, and maybe we could find some weed along the way," he laughingly added. "I really need some...I mean, with all this stress. It's been way too long." Private McCree enlisted in the air force as a way to escape jail time for bringing three joints from Mexico into Texas. He would have done anything not to have to go to jail.

At eleven-thirty P.M., the two boys left their hut, trudging through swampy fields until they arrived at their opening in the fence. They were weak from not eating or drinking much. When the two privates ripped the fence open, a succession of bullets sounded through the night. They were killed instantly. It seems the rip in the fence was placed there on purpose to tempt the prisoners. It worked, and now all that were left were four.

Another three weeks passed until, one rainy afternoon, the Hanoians made four nooses and hung them four feet apart from each other. The four Americans knew what the enemy wanted at that point. Two of the remaining soldiers pleaded on their hands and knees to be let go. The Vietcongs strung these two fellows up first. The two remaining captives knew there was no other way out. They had to chance escape while the enemy was performing the two executions.

Forgetting where he was positioned, the nervous sergeant ran in the opposite direction of the hole. Kenneth instinctively ran toward the hole, jumping over creeks and marshy areas. Now he was really wishing that he had participated in that Olympic qualification track meet his father had suggested he enter and train for. "My father was always right," he said to himself as he jumped and straddled deep ravines which held muddy rainwater, fearing for his life the entire time. "This sure enough brought me vulnerability, it made me more down to earth, but I don't know about the toughness part."

Kenneth made it to the fence in record time, crawling through the sharp, broken ended barbed-wire pieces that surrounded the wide hole. As he dragged his final body part through the jagged opening, he heard a shot ring through the fields. "Dammit, those bastards got the sergeant," Kenneth yelled, hearing his echo resounding in the distance.

* * *

Francis worked as the cook in the Irish restaurant for three and a half years before beginning a decade of moving from town to town—always near Boston, however. He stayed in a one-room apartment in Beverly for three years, but after this, he rented one month at a time in each small town, never getting bored in stagnation. Francis loved living life as a gypsy.

One night, while at a local dive near Revere Beach where he was living at the time, he met two girls. One of the girls was named Tina. She sheepishly said, "My name is Tina, and I'm from Holsbrook. Where are you from?"

Francis answered nonchalantly, glancing around the room, then at this woman, who he thought had pleasant but rather ordinary looks. "I'm from everywhere."

Tina said, "Ya know, ya look and sound just like a former boyfriend of mine from high school."

Francis said in a snappy way, "Okay...what's his name?"

"Kenneth Redman," she replied. "A doll—and very rich." She drunkenly slurred, "He was so lucky he got adopted into that life. He had everything...had every girl you could ever imagine...just made of gold. Kenny was pretty cold-hearted, though. Had too much going for him. Just too much ego...but I liked him, still."

Francis' ears perked up. He wondered, had he hit the jackpot? He excitedly told the girls he had to go. He had business to take care of in the morning.

The provocatively-dressed Tina slipped her phone number into Francis' rugged hand and whispered softly into his ear, "Call me sometime."

He nodded and walked out of the bar to his apartment, where he was to plan his quiet attack. The next afternoon Francis drove to Holsbrook, went to the county records office, and told the officials there of his relentless desire to meet his twin. He informed the workers that the two were supposedly separated at birth. He found out that Kenneth Redman was born on his own birthday, in the same year, and in the same orphanage. This was the break for which he had been waiting. There was no current address for Kenneth, however, only the address of Kenneth's parents at the time of his birth.

Francis walked out of the office with a smile, thinking, *Well, at least I'm getting somewhere.* He revved up his small but powerful engine and left the county municipality, heading over the creek and up the street until he arrived at 508 Arbor Lane Drive, as the address read. He turned onto the cracked driveway of the overgrown plot of land, which displayed what looked like a large gingerbread house, in great need of repair, situated smack dab in the middle of disarrayed foliage. Francis got out of his vehicle hesitantly and proceeded to begin the investigation into his twin's life.

* * *

Kenneth got through the Vietnam War with honors. He was promoted to major and sent to Germany. He stayed in Munich for close to five years, conducting routine practice missions throughout Western Europe, until he had enough. He requested one week off to simply go back to his home in Massachusetts and visit his father, who was very ill. This request was denied by his commanding general, General Bryant. When he got the news, Kenneth went straight to the nearest bar and had several *biers* with several *frauleins* who took him upstairs. When he awoke with a pounding headache, he said *auf wiedersehen* to the *damen* and got a taxi home, where he begin to plan his getaway to the states.

As soon as he opened the door to his apartment, he ran to the kitchen to phone several of his officers and tell each what he wanted him to do. Kenneth requested a military jet, orders, and clearance papers, which he found could be arranged through General Smythe, who he had flown with in Vietnam.

When General Bryant found out about Smythe's overriding of his own denial, he tried to get Smythe court marshaled. Bryant couldn't accomplish this, however, because of both Smythe's and Redman's impeccable military records. Two days later, Kenneth's appeal for temporary leave was granted, so he flew to Boston. He bunked with his father in his private hospital room. Kenneth had stayed there for only one week when Thomas got cold and blue and died of pneumonia. Kenneth would have given up his entire military career just to be with his hero at this end. Kenneth had become a very heroic and respected man, a far cry from what he had been as a teen.

Kenneth requested an extended leave in order to get the estate affairs in order, as he was the executor. He was granted this request. At the reading of the will, Kenneth was to receive five million dollars. His mother was to receive the other five million and the home. Kenneth's mother, Kate, who was in her sixties herself, put Kenneth in her will as the sole beneficiary.

It was during this leave that he met his only wife, Jane.

* * *

Francis got a call late one evening, while fixing a pot of homemade chili with plenty of diced onions and shredded sharp cheddar. He had the six o'clock news cranked up while he sizzled sirloin on the stove. This was his usual "day-off" meal, and he looked forward to it with passion, enjoying every moment of its preparation. Chili, chips, and Guinness was his favorite anecdote to a busy week.

Standing his large spoon in the pot of thick chili, he picked up the wall phone and immediately stood at attention when he heard a deep voiced man loudly say, almost shouting, "Hello, this is Anthony Farres, maitre'd, and I'm with Countess Cruises." He inquisitively asked, "Is this Francis Cranford?"

Francis replied, "At your service."

Anthony bluntly told Francis that the cruise line was interviewing for the position of head chef on their Mediterranean runs. They needed a highly qualified master chef for the two ships that worked a two week total run. The cruise line had received several recommendations on Francis' gourmet cuisines. Sounding direct, Anthony stated, "Both are hard runs, very demanding, but they will make your pockets stretch out." He continued, "The first ship leaves Barcelona on Saturday and continues to Palma de Mallorca, Marseilles, Monaco, and Florence, disembarking in Rome the next Saturday. From there the second ship leaves Rome for Sicily, Athens, Santorini, and Istanbul, from Saturday to Saturday as well." He clarified that the run was scheduled from October through May; the base pay was seventy-five thousand dollars a year. Anthony quickly added, without a breath, "And of course, the head chef gets tipped in a major way, if the job is done well, because only wealthy guests board our elegant ships. And, by the way," he inserted, "our chef is given lavish room and board." Smiling from cheek to cheek, Francis agreed to an interview the very next morning at ten at the cruise line headquarters in Providence.

"This is the break I've been waiting for!" he screamed throughout his apartment as he reached into his fridge, took out the cheap bottle of bubbly—saved for a special occasion like this one, or a cheap date—and popped the cork. Pink champagne spewed everywhere. Francis just laughed hysterically and drank the whole bottle while cooking his chili.

The next morning he awoke with a start, looked at the clock, and saw it was only four, not five, for which Francis had originally set the alarm. He got up anyway, made himself a single cup of java, and sleepily cooked up some hot oatmeal from scratch. He thought this to be the perfect breakfast, one that was small and light enough to keep him energized all morning while not weighing him down for the drive or the interview ahead. He poured whole milk over the steamy oats and mixed in one teaspoon of brown sugar and one of butter. Francis quickly ate, then finished his coffee, which had a touch of espresso mixed in to get him going in the mornings. Then he got ready in the bathroom and decided what apparel would be appropriate for a master chef interview. He had never been on an interview like this; he had mostly worked in dives up and down the coast of Massachusetts where it didn't matter how he dressed. Francis quickly decided on a tan and green, long-sleeved, striped polo shirt with khaki pants and deck shoes. He thought to himself, *This makes me look rock solid and confident...the perfect combination to get what you want in life.*

He made it to Providence in what seemed to be record time, probably because during the entire ride he was thinking about his twin and how he might meet up with him and his money. After finding the fancy three-story brick building in the center of town, Francis carefully climbed out of his used two-door jalopy, which displayed a new coat of slate grey sparkles. It did have a good working engine. The car had never let him down. He reached into his back pocket to get the information Anthony had recited to him the day before, and that is when he found it...Tina's phone number. He thought that he must not have worn his khakis since that evening he met her at the bar since he mostly wore his faded jeans. Francis felt this to be an omen and promised himself, "If I get this job, I'm gonna take this female to the Ritz for drinks, food, and sex...that way, I can find out more about my brother."

He had not been able to find out anything about his brother's whereabouts except that he was a high-ranking officer stationed somewhere in Europe. He had found this information by talking to the Redman's former neighbors, who lived next to the ginger bread house. The Baby Boomer neighbors had seen Francis through their window and darted over that day, asking how they could help him. This couple informed him that the Redmans had moved from there about ten years ago. Francis asked them if they knew to where the family had moved. The man and woman shook their heads and told him that the Redmans were said to have moved to a very large house located on a few acres outside of town in the countryside. They had also heard that Mr. Redman had been in and out of hospitals over the past year. He evidently was in a perpetual state of illness. Francis was not able to receive any more information about his twin from that chance encounter. He knew what he should be concentrating on now: the large house near the edge of town and when he was going to talk to Mr. and Mrs. Redman.

Francis told the elderly, but seemingly competent, receptionist in the lobby that he had an appointment with Anthony Farres at ten. She buzzed the maitre'd upstairs, and in what seemed like two minutes, a rather large, jovial, dark brown haired and skinned Italian, with a rosy round face and menacing grey eyes, came out from behind the elevator doors. He said, "Follow me," in a take charge manner as he led the way down the black marbled hallway until it dead-ended into a dreary, boxy conference room. It did provide some comfort that nervous Francis craved, however, as the stale room looked out onto a elaborate Japanese garden with small wooden bridges. Here Francis showed Anthony photos of some of his flamboyant concoctions, along with several dessert samples he carried in a tupperware dish. Anthony was impressed by everything, especially Francis' confident demeanor. The maitre'd thought to himself, as Francis raved on and on about his dishes and how much the patrons loved them, *This might be the guy we need.* He had not been able to find the right replacement for their former head chef, who had left three years before due to illness. The others had been too thin-skinned for all of the criticism and pompousness they had to tolerate on a daily basis. In general, the snooty clientele seemed to be getting harder and harder to please. *Francis might be the guy to pass my complaints and requests on to. Why not? He'd be the new kid on the block, and he needs to be broken-in,* Anthony rationalized to himself, strategizing all of his moves while wrinkling his forehead.

Francis had never felt like a big shot before the night when he got Anthony's all-important call. Now he felt special, like some former angel was looking out for him, showing him where he should go and what he should become. He was feeling powerful and manipulative, deceitful and dirty.

Anthony called Francis the following morning at nine sharp and told him Countess Cruise Lines was prepared to offer him the head chef position. Elated, but not wanting to appear too excited, Francis calmly told him, "Sure, I'll take it. Why not?" Paperwork was sent back and forth between the two parties.

Francis was scheduled to depart for Greece in one month, in October. With only three days left, he made sure he had gotten all of his affairs in order, and he had, except for one. When he again saw her name and phone number, this time lying on top of his dresser, he decided to give it a chance and ring her. "I have nothing to lose, and lots to gain," he whispered to himself.

"What's up?" the tall, auburn-haired Tina asked in her sultry voice as she picked up the receiver, seeing Francis' name on caller I.D. "It took you a long time to give me a shout. How's come? You don't like me or sumpin'?"

"No, I like you fine...just fine," Francis murmured inaudibly.

"What? Can't hear nuttin'!" she interrupted.

Speaking louder, Francis restated, "Of course I like ya. Otherwise I wouldn't of called you to ask you on a date tonight."

"Tonight?" Tina asked, perking up. "When? And where?"

"Eight o'clock at the Ritz Carlton," he replied.

"Wow, did you strike it rich or something, babe?" Tina asked, smirking.

"Well, sort of. I'll tell you about it later. How's 'bout we meet at the bar in front, then go to dinner from there? You never know what might happen after that, toots," Francis indiscreetly added. He knew she was a loose broad, so he didn't have to worry about play-acting with her. He also surmised that she was lying about knowing Kenneth in high school. She had probably been a "pro," and he a "john" when they met, maybe even on numerous occasions.

"What you see, my fiery, slutty Tina, is what you get! And you for sure want me. It's obvious!" he sang in a made-up, mundane, two-note melody.

After three very strong, salty martinis, the two decided to get a room and order room service. Francis ordered beef tips and rice cooked in a mushroom wine sauce and an asparagus soufflé. For dessert they had cherries jubilee and strong black coffee waiting on the huge round tray, placed on a stand by the dinner table.

Tina didn't have dining etiquette—or really any etiquette at all, for that matter. She complained about heartburn from the mushroom sauce with every bite. She didn't even try the soufflé, said it looked awful and that she hated vegetables. She only ate the vanilla ice cream, scraping off the fancy liqueur and sweet cherries from the cherries jubilee. She couldn't stand the taste or smell of coffee either. She said she drank ice tea with saccharin in the mornings. Since gourmet dining experiences were so important to Frances, and a part of his being, Tina proved very boring to him from the start.

After this disastrous candlelit celebration, Francis decided to load some Sinatra into his portable compact disc player, hoping it might lift his spirits so that he might find the information he wanted so desperately. He seemed to get side-tracked, however, about why he had even asked her out in the first place when Tina unexpectedly took off her busty, transparent, long-sleeved spandex shirt, which he had stared a hole through the entire evening. She then pulled off Francis' sweater and started licking his hairy, muscular chest. Moaning, he lifted her skirt and massaged her private parts, then took her from the chair and carried her into the bedroom alcove. It was apparent she was merely a sexual toy to him. The love of sex was the only thing he had in common with her and the only thing that Francis even liked about the girl. She reached many orgasmic heights throughout their session. He did too, but only through oral sex, which was his favorite, by far. She seemed a bitch to him, and a serious nymphomaniac, but in his horny state, he didn't care.

At midnight Tina silently got out of bed, dressed, and left the room without even leaving a note. When he awoke at eight-fifteen, Francis was panic-stricken. He did not even know where she lived or worked. He called her number, which was still on top of the dresser, and heard only a three-note melody on the other end, followed by a computerized recording of a female's voice saying, "The number you have dialed has been disconnected." The only leads he had on where to find her were the Revere Beach bars where she supposedly hung out.

He banged his head on the wall, thinking about what a stupid fool he had been the previous night. He had not even had the chance to ask her if she knew Kenneth's parents and their address. No, nothing was accomplished. She had gotten the best of him, and he had gotten *nada*, except for an expensive evening with a cheap dame. "The dame would have cost less at a bordello—and probably been more sophisticated," Francis said out loud to himself.

The following afternoon he went up and down the beach questioning establishment workers as to whether or not any knew the girl, giving her name and description. They all said they'd never known or seen anyone like that, except for one old time proprietor at Greensleeves, an English club across from the beach. He told Francis, "Yeah, I know her, have known her since she was a young stripper in Springfield. She was never any good. She lived in ill-repute houses since she was about seventeen. She never went to school, never really had a family, just an alcoholic mother and a deadbeat father who left them both to marry a dancer from Paris. She would always come around and try to sell her 'product' for money whenever the rent was due. I'm warning ya, bud, stay away from her."

Francis asked, excitedly, "But did she ever go to Holsbrook High?"

"Are you kiddin'?" was all the old man uttered as he glared in disbelief. "She never even made it to high school," he continued as he made his way to the entrance to open up shop.

Francis knew then he had been had for sure, and he left the establishment angrily taunting himself. He repeated, "You should have been smarter and abstained.

41

You're better than that. If you ever see her again, it's definitely lights out for the scanky dame."

* * *

Kenneth again saw the pretty hazel-eyed girl with ash brown hair at the shop where he always picked up postcards to send to his officer buddies. Not thinking he stood a chance, he approached her nervously at the counter.

Surprisingly, she blurted out, "Hi, I'm Jane, if you need any help."

"Thanks," he shyly replied. Slightly batting her eyelashes at him, she aggressively said, "You know, I've seen you here many times before and always wished you'd talk to me. You haven't until now, but we still have time."

Kenneth flirtatiously responded, "Time for what, dear?"

Jane cunningly answered, "For whatever life has in store for us, hon." She looked into Kenneth's dark grey eyes and asked, looking provocative, "You wanna go out on a date sometime?"

That evening, when she got off work, he met her at the shop and they went to an open-aired café on the fishing pier in Camden, where they both had Maine lobster and coffee and brandy. They instantly fell in love with each other as they laughed together in the foggy moonlight of early September.

Jane and Kenneth dated for two years before getting married. She had just turned twenty-three; he was still thirty-eight when they took their vows. They lived in a large four-bedroom, two and a half bath home on the outskirts of Holsbrook, near his mother and located on three wooded acres. It was a nice retreat for Kenneth, when he returned from England on a bi-weekly basis, to spend four days in his "kingdom," with his faithful young wife. They had many good friends, parties, and possessions, but only a fair marriage from the start.

Kenneth's mother died when Kenneth was forty-one. She had had a long bout with brain cancer. Kenneth and Jane moved into the inherited estate right before he served Jane with divorce papers.

Not knowing how to behave in a committed relationship, as he had never really been in one, not in his entire life, not even in a true friendship, he did not give his fair share to the marriage. He had only used people for his own wants and desires. This was why Kenneth thought that he, himself, had ruined the marriage. Kenneth had never been there for Jane, not even when he had physically been beside her. Never had his mind been on his wife, only on himself. In his pursuance of victory, he earned and accomplished more and more, but never once did he include Jane in any of these pursuits. He never really included her in anything, for that matter. After reaching his final rank of two-star general, he became very aloof and contemplative whenever Jane came near him. He had been given huge responsibilities and challenges in Europe during their marriage, and he became a mastermind in military air strategies. When he was promoted to general at a huge soiree, Jane wasn't even in attendance. The celebration was in England, and she was in Holsbrook. He didn't even inform her of the occasion or ask her to be his escort. Thinking of this event, he drunkenly told her, while guzzling brandy late one night, "You are far too good for me and deserve better." He said he had always thought that.

They divorced two and a half years later, and he knew that he had done Jane wrong. He told her so in a long letter. He was slowly being lifted, by the hand of God, up from the heat.

* * *

Francis didn't have time to delve into his brother's existence. He was now ready to depart for his job of a lifetime, ready to make some cash and have some fun. He didn't care now. He put his sibling on the back burner. "I don't care if I ever meet the rat bastard, 'cause I don't need him, never needed him in the first place. He's probably bogus, anyway, ya know? Doesn't even have a dime to his name...I'm the cool one now." Francis whispered this soliloquy to the flight magazine he was reading while crossing the Atlantic.

Chapter Seven

Francis jumped up the next morning with a start, thinking his twin was standing before him, staring at him. All night long, he had had a very restless sleep in which he tossed and turned, dreaming about twenty-year-old cruise ship scenarios.

Right before he woke, he had one of his on-going Mafia nightmares. He had begun to have these nightmares when he started work at the beach pub. Many of the clientele there belonged to the Irish Mafia. Francis heard about all of their escapades over brews and became very good chums with all of them. They would sometimes close up the bar together, all becoming inebriated. A few days earlier, Hugo Henry, one of the most respected of the Irish mobsters, made an entrance at the pub. Hugo was born in Belfast but raised as a teenager in Boston. He was the son of the most famous criminal mind in the British Isles, Patrick Z. Henry. Hugo and his mother, Maddie, moved to Boston to begin a new existence when Patrick Z. was placed in the confines of a Northern Irish penitentiary. Maddie was tired of the constant ups and downs of living life with her good-looking but unstable Patrick. He was a perpetual playboy and renegade.

Hugo had also been a renegade all of his life. He coolly and suavely glided through life, wherever and whenever. All heads turned to look whenever he entered an establishment. He had a tremendous ego, as everyone could tell. He felt he could do anything to anyone, without any repercussions. His four ex-wives had each testified to that trait of his personality at their divorce hearings. They all said Hugo had bedazzled them with his kindness at first, winning their trust and affection—then *bam*, he changed overnight and become an egocentric mad man.

Hugo walked over to Francis, smiled mischievously, and placed his finger on Francis' upper cheek, tracing a squarish circle over his blemished area, Francis uncomfortably backed away, his mouth open in bewilderment as if he wanted to say something but could not. Taking one last swig of his pint, Hugo smirked, "When are you gonna take care of that, boy? You've been wearing that since your cruise days."

Francis laughed, "Well, how can I, bloke? It's permanent...from birth. Hey, don't I know you or something?"

Hugo said, "Nah," and scribbled something on one of the bar napkins, pushing it down the bar to Francis.

Francis asked, "What's this shit?"

"Call the number and see for yourself...but it will make your life change," Hugo said, wild-eyed, as he flung his jacket over his shoulder and waltzed out of the pub.

* * *

When the alarm clock, which laid on a pile of much-read recipe books, began to belt out tunes from the "nifty-fifties," Francis got himself up to make his morning one-cup of sanity. He learned a unique way of fixing a mug of piping hot java from Mr. O'Sullivan, without a percolator. He cupped one industrial-strength paper towel, filled with ground coffee beans, and placed it over his mug. He then boiled water in a tea pot and poured this water through the paper towel, over the ground coffee, and into the mug. The strong aroma of steaming, fresh, robust brown liquid quickly filled the room. This was the easiest, most efficient, and least costly way to start the day for him. Only when he had a date, or a dinner party with friends, was this method not functional.

He saw the number that the Irish dude had written on the napkin, which Francis had placed on the kitchen counter by the stove. He dialed the number on the napkin and waited for over ten rings until a perky voice answered the call, "Facial surgery with Dr. Martin." Francis hung up the phone. *What the hell?* he thought.

Five minutes later, there was a forceful banging at the saloon door as Francis was dressing in the apartment he rented upstairs. He walked downstairs into the bar to see what was wanted this early in the morning. Francis looked down the sidewalk, squinting through the latched chain. He saw Hugo standing there, wearing a sly smile on the left side of his fair-skinned face. Hugo's salt-and-pepper hair looked as if it badly needed a trimming, and Francis thought the bald spot on the back of his head to be getting bigger by the moment. Annoyed, Francis unlatched the door and asked Hugo what he wanted this early. Hugo handed him a white box with a black ribbon on it. Hugo looked at Francis and exclaimed, "Well, what are you waiting for? Open it!" As Francis did this, his expression changed from annoyance to astonishment.

In the box was more money than Francis had ever before seen, along with a card underneath the pile that read, "This is to remove your birthmark with Dr. Martin, along with a stash of recoup dough. Call Martin to make an appointment, and listen to me, Fran. I'm the one you answer to now."

Back upstairs, Francis found the crumpled up napkin on the floor by the garbage can and unraveled it. He dialed the number once again, but this time he spoke with the perky-voiced girl on the other end. He asked her how she was, and she said, "Very hot, thank you." He smiled to himself and asked if she could squeeze him in sometime soon to see Dr. Martin about a birthmark scar removal.

She asked, "How's about tomorrow afternoon, sweetie?"

Unsure about how he got an appointment that quickly, Francis robotically answered, "Perfect."

* * *

After waiting the following afternoon for nearly an hour, flirting with the blonde, bubble gum-chewing receptionist, who wore red spiked heels on her high-arched dancer feet, a clingy white tank top, and black low-riders, a red-headed pudgy middle-aged man in a long white jacket and green scrubs entered the room where Francis sat at a long conference table. The man introduced himself as Doc Martin, facial surgery specialist.

The doc immediately took sight of his abnormality and assuredly nodded and said, "This should be no problem. I'll have you looking like a million bucks by tomorrow."

"Tomorrow?" Francis asked.

The doc replied, "The boys want it done the sooner the better, so I'll make it my first priority of the day. Be here tomorrow morning at nine," and he abruptly left the room.

"Wow," Francis murmured to himself. "What is going on here?"

For some reason, at that moment he again thought about the twin he wanted so desperately to meet and about his chance encounter with Tina at the dump on the beach. He had been thinking a lot about his brother lately, so he had decided the first thing he was going to do after he healed was find his twin.

And did that ever happen. Francis didn't know what was in store for himself, or what he was about to turn into.

* * *

When he got up at six the following morning, so he could get to the doc's clinic at nine, he walked into the cozy kitchen and remembered he wasn't supposed to drink anything or nibble on anything, not even the tasty banana bread he had made the day earlier. He phoned the restaurant and told them the doc said it might be a few days until he could return to the hot kitchen. The restaurant asked that Francis just drop off some of the new lobster sandwich recipes he had concocted and which everyone seemed to adore. The stuffed lobster roll had become the favorite at the beach bar.

Francis had served Countess Cruises well over a twenty-five year period. Many thought he had been the best master chef the line had ever had. Francis had all the females, and even a few of the males, wanting to go up to his balcony suite for the night. He had become such a con artist because of this entire experience. He was by no means rich, though, even though he did bring home a healthy paycheck. He had acquired no assets, as well as no liabilities, during his employment. He had lived his life up until now like there was no tomorrow.

At the ripe age of sixty-five, he finally felt he needed a rest. He was becoming less energetic and more tired of his monotonous routine. Plus, his fan base was dwindling. He now looked and felt like a worn out rag. He told his best friend, Anthony, about his decision to retire from the cruise line. Tony understood and thought it best, too.

It was on his last two-week run that he met a striking, dark Irishman, about forty years old, named Hugo. They became acquaintances on board ship for the week as they talked about Boston, about Ireland, and of their Irish backgrounds and their Bostonian hangouts. They exchanged email addresses but never kept in touch.

On that last bittersweet morning when docking in the Port of Piraneus, Francis packed his bags, picked up his last paycheck, cashed it on board, and disembarked from the ship...forever. He flew from Athens to Boston and went straight to his old Revere Beach hangout, where he was greeted royally. He was offered a full-time cooking job there his first day back, which he accepted, and he worked there for the next three years. He felt like himself again...down and dirty, lean and mean. He felt good, wearing his old faded jeans and muscle shirt, and cooking his favorite...lobster rolls. He was still toned, for a man of his age, as he ran the beach and lifted weights daily. The cruise ship had provided him lots of opportunities to meet plenty of fancy, moneyed people, but again, that scene wasn't really him. Long-term commitments with prestigious men and women never interested Francis, only pushed him away—far away. He had to have his space, freedom, and smut.

He strolled into the clinic a little after nine after hurriedly giving the recipe copies to the part-time cooks. The nurses rushed him into a laboratory to test him for any allergies and check his pulse before they put him under anesthesia. He was in good physical condition, tests showed, except for an occasional heart murmur, which could be a problem if left unguarded. He had an unknown allergy to penicillin, which they took care to note in their records. Having this crucial information, the anesthesiologists began to place tubes and needles in his arm. "One hundred, ninety-nine, ninety-eight, ninety-seven, ninety-six, ninety-five...," he muttered to himself before falling asleep.

* * *

When his eyes opened three hours later, there were five of Francis's friends from the mob surrounding his bed. They were supposed to take him back to his apartment and make sure he was comfortable. The boys were really catering to him. He wondered why. He struggled to get up out of the bed, with the help of the boys and one mousy, brown bouffant-headed, petite nurse. They walked with him over to the bathroom where he dressed so that he was able to leave the clinic. He splashed cold water on his face, and he felt ready to go and see what was in store for him.

The doc came into the room and said that everything had gone well and that Francis should be able to take the bandage off of his face in seven days. The mob boys then escorted him to a waiting limo and drove him instead to one of the boys' estates, near the harbor. *This must be where they're gonna talk to me*, Francis thought.

Francis now started getting tense and worried as he saw the emotionless, sullen looks on each of the mob boys' faces. As they started walking down the flower-laced brick pathway leading up to the massive mahogany front doors, Hugo emerged. He said, "I'm glad you could join us all in one piece after your surgery. It's now time you listened to what we have to say. Come inside, and please, please make yourself comfortable, and we'll tell you what we expect from you." Francis sauntered inside with the others.

The boys got extra pillows and propped up Francis on the elegant mauve velvet sofa, and Francis comfortably heard the details of their elaborate scheme. Hugo revealed the entire plot. He told Francis that he was to double as his twin brother, Kenneth Redman, in order to get vital information and take Kenneth's place in society.

Francis freaked, looking down at the ground, and said, "You mean, this is how I'll finally get to meet him?"

"I suppose you're wondering why, ain't ya, Fran?" asked Hugo.

"Just tell me what you're trying to get from me killing my twin brother," Francis barked in amazement,

"Just tell me, what's the real deal?"

Hugo answered, "The real deal is that you got half a million dollars in a box to kill your brother. Over the next few months, you are to trace each of his steps and moves, get to know his friends and acquaintances, and all about his businesses, clients, and bank accounts. When the time is right, a ten million dollar life insurance policy on Francis Cranford will be taken out by his twin brother Kenneth Redman, with Doc Martin's written A+ evaluation of Francis' health."

"I still don't understand," Francis blurted out.

"Oh, you will," Hugo grinned and began the drama. He pointed his finger at Francis and lectured, "You, Francis Cranford, alias Kenneth Redman, will receive a red hot check for ten million dollars, and you will in turn give us all proceeds. You see, Francis Cranford has mysteriously died from a misdiagnosis, with wrong drugs being administered and prescribed to him. You will be the one who gets into Kenneth's manor home to switch pills in two bottles and begin pumping poison into his veins. We'll arm you with a stun gun to knock him out so you can give him that first dose. After that, it's all downhill, except you have to bring him to us. You think you can do it?" Hugo asked. He quickly added, "For a job well done, there's also a hefty bonus. It's fuckin' easy....you don't even know the old geezer."

Francis immediately said, "You know I'll do it." His soul had definitely now been transferred into one of the devil's clutches.

Francis counted down the next seven days almost in desperation. He called Dr. Martin's secretary on the third day and told her of his intense pain. Even with the black market pain killers given to him, they weren't killing the agony, just making him woozy and light-headed. He wanted the doc to know this and call him back. The doc did this right after his scheduled surgical procedure. The doctor told him to take those pills with a glass of brandy if they weren't working. He added, "You need to acquire a taste for brandy, anyway, if you're going to portray Kenneth. You know, he really loves the stuff, became dependent on it. I've never seen anyone who had such important responsibilities become so addicted." He stressed, "Pills and brandy are a dangerous mix, so please be careful."

On the fifth day, he felt much better. The highly-dosed codeine and brandy made a surprisingly potent concoction. He slept like a baby for two nights. On the sixth day, the pain had gone completely. On the day of unveiling, Francis was ready to see if the doctor's magical reputation and skill rang true.

Before Francis started, he downed a shot of brandy so that he would feel no pain when he ripped off the surgical tape. The cotton gauze that covered his left cheek was attached to the skin by what seemed to be a type of gluey ointment. Now was the time of reckoning. Would it be a miracle, or a disaster? He ripped off the bandage.

Chapter Eight

Francis gently tugged at the cloth, lifting it up at its edges. Keeping his eyes shut, he took the covering off. Francis took another swig of his newfound pain remedy, brandy, before opening his eyes. He let the brandy trickle down his trachea, then popped his eyes wide open, as if in a horror flick. He gawked at what he saw.

He traced where the blemished lines were in the mirror from memory, because they were there no more—not a trace. Some pinkness and swelling protruded slightly from the upper part of the cheek, but it looked as if he had simply bumped into something.

He called the doc to report in and tell him about the protrusion, but he was in surgery. Again, Francis left a message for the doc with Kathy, the hot receptionist. Doc Martin called him back three and a half hours later. He told Francis that he knew the procedure would turn out perfect. "I'm good," he stated. "Some even say I'm great. All I do is my job the best way I know how. And about the pinkness and the swelling—well, that's normal. It's just irritated from the surgical shock on that very fragile, sensitive area. I had to be particularly careful with the eye being so close to where I was working. I'm glad it looks perfect, but I knew it would. And with that, I'll dismiss you from my care, unless you run into a problem, which you shouldn't. I have other matters to tend to now."

Francis knew to what he was referring, and he left the conversation alone. He assumed that Doc Martin had a thriving business, judging from his expertise, and that he did this kind of funny stuff on the side for a lot of extra dough. It's not like he didn't already have millions, but he wanted more. *What a greedy son-of-a-bitch*, he thought to himself, before bidding him *adieu*.

Francis called Hugo after he hung up and gave him the news. Hugo sent a limo for Francis to come to the estate, where pictures and film of Kenneth's dealings were to be displayed in the basement. When Francis arrived, the mob boys had champagne flowing, plenty of pretty girls in tight mini-skirts, and a blues band wailing in the backyard. Everyone was amazed at the sight of Francis's face.

The scent of Ben Franklins filled the air.

Francis looked at an array of photos and film clips. These included Kenneth's meetings with dignitaries in the United States Air Force, along with government officials from other lands. Kenneth appeared very smooth and gracious in all of these social affairs. As far as business meetings were concerned, which were displayed next, he appeared very stern, astute, and patient, yet hurried at the same time.

There was a client of his in one sharply defined photograph with whom he seemed jovial, almost flirtatious. This client was the rich cosmetic queen herself, Cassie Cay. The picture was taken at her ranch, near Ocala, Florida. Francis was then played a tape which was dubbed into a sequence of film clips of one of their conversations taken from the chips placed on Kenneth's watch link and motor vehicle. Kenneth spoke quickly and directly to her, but in a playful manner. He obviously enjoyed doing business with Cassie, but who wouldn't? Cassie was a distinguished looking multi-millionaire who owned a prestigious estate located off the interstate heading south to Tampa. Cassie appeared to be a trifle older than Kenneth. She was tall and slim and still in good muscular shape. She had long, shiny, black hair which she twirled on top of her almond-shaped head. She placed only two long bobby pins in her hair to keep it secure. She constantly bragged about this. She had very defined facial features and naturally red lips. She wasn't stunning, but she had a unique look that attracted men. She had a dramatic way about her, and although she was elegant and refined in social life, she was rough and tough in business. Kenneth liked this.

Kenneth sold her two mares, shoved the cash in the pocket of his tight cowboy jeans, and began to walk down the hill toward the gate of the estate, where his Escalade was parked. Cassie briskly walked with him, her shivering arms folded, looking to the east for the sun to fully rise and provide some warmth on this chilly early February morning. She pointed to the right of where they were standing and said, "This is where Becca McClain, the famous country singer, is going to build her second home. She bought five acres from me last week. She's supposed to put in a recording studio out back. It'll be a pretty busy place around here when she gets her palace built and moves in."

Kenneth said dryly, as he climbed into his transport, "Until next time, Cassie. See ya," and gave her a wink, followed by a salute. Cassie was obviously saddened by his departure, but she revived herself when she heard the phone ringing from afar. She galloped up the front walkway, like one of her race horses, desperate to get to the house before the ringing ceased. She had been waiting for an important call regarding a special ingredient that supposedly kept lipstick on the mouth, never smearing. This was how she kept in such good shape for her age— by walking, running, and horseback riding throughout her extensive property. She wished Kenneth would get off his ass and ask her out on a date. Cassie knew they'd be great together; they were both attractive, both thought alike, and both lived life in grand style. Cassie also gave a tremendous amount of her earnings to an assortment of charities, mostly for children, as did Kenneth. Kenneth and Cassie especially loved children, but they religiously helped anyone in need.

* * *

Francis ordered a tall brandy from the gorgeous, orange-haired, busty playmate who was taking bar orders with a foreign accent. As he was contemplating the entire situation, Hugo nudged him in his funny bone. Hugo showed him more photos of Kenneth's boys who manage the apartment complex for him, and who, of course, drink with him nightly at several of the small, seedy taverns on Central Avenue. They looked like a goofy, intoxicated bunch. He saw clips of his twin and his buddies mooning female bar patrons while these heavily made-up customers were displaying their boobs back at them. Francis wondered how Kenneth could have gotten so far in life behaving like this. "There's no audio or film on this set of characters," Hugo interjected. "Just photos, bios, and applications with personal information that should be helpful in getting to know the cast and where they come from."

Hugo gave Francis illegally-retrieved financial statements from the general's LLC and all the cast's personal affairs. Judging from these records, Chase McCarty was the most professional, and definitely the most moneyed. He was the general manager of several small "in need of refurbishment" apartment buildings in the downtown area of St. Pete, which were all owned by Kenneth, bought at very low prices, and which made hundreds of thousands of dollars yearly from rental revenue. He had hired the other two cast members, by the names of Peter Sciara and Blaine Hampton. Hugo recited his spiel, "Peter is said to wash clothing for the accounting department. Even though he is a supposed jerk and a know-it-all, Peter knows how to hide money well. He came from an upper-middle class family in Queens; his dad was a pediatrician. They sent Peter to Yale, and he majored in international finance. Peter lived on the Spanish Mediterranean for seven years, where he worked in a major bank with American customers. He never felt comfortable there because he couldn't get a handle on the language, so he returned to the States when he was thirty. He then got a job as a broker with a mortgage company, as merely a consultant. Peter was next offered a job as a vice-president of an up and coming brokerage firm, as a vice-president in the mortgage department. He took this position in a heartbeat and stayed there until he took early retirement. He had accumulated a couple million dollars, and he thought this plenty to start the quiet life he had always wanted to lead. Kenneth was Peter's bar buddy at one of the places in downtown St. Pete. Kenneth asked him, when he first acquired the place, if he'd be interested in working at the complex part-time. Peter said yes, and part-time soon turned into full-time.

"The Internal Revenue Service audited Kenneth's books three times in the last ten years, but found no wrong-doings," Hugo rambled on, changing the topic. "Kenneth has so many investments, properties, cars used for business, and a multitude of other deductions, that he and his LLC appeared to be in the red two out of the three years. For the third audited year, Kenneth only showed a slight profit and had to pay a minimal amount to the government. He was clean and always had been. He enjoys drinking and being loud and rowdy, but that is as far as it goes with Ken. He likes living life on the up and up, never having to look over his shoulder," he continued matter of factly.

"And as far as Blaine is concerned, he's a nice chump, birthed from British parents who immigrated over the Atlantic to Philadelphia on a freighter in the mid-sixties, immediately after their wedding at a church in the Cotswalds. His father worked in all types of jobs until he found his calling in ship building. He became a ship builder for the Coast Guard in Philly. Blaine was born several years later. His father was then transferred to the Coast Guard station in St. Pete Bay five years later, where he worked until his retirement. Blaine calls St. Petersburg his home. He attended ten years of school there until he got a wild hair at the age of sixteen to join a rock band and go on the road. The band never made it, never even paid its bills. The members had to work two and three jobs to even exist in the industry. One day, Hugo reported, "the lead singer was found shot to death in a gas station restroom. Supposedly it was suicide, and that was the end of Blaine's music career." Hugo said that Blaine learned the construction trade after that. "He lives a simple life downtown but always has steady work. He works on the apartment complex when they need him."

Chapter Nine

Hugo had gotten more intense and more animated with the expounding of each new character in the scenario. He was now at edge of his fold-out lawn chair that he kept in his cabana permanently, alongside a long, rectangular white painted table with chipped paint on its edges and, adjacent to that, another lawn chair, where Francis sat, awaiting an explanation. Hugo had never looked more serious than when he stared at Francis and ranted," It's been over three days, and now I feel is the time we've been waiting for...to tell you why we have to acquaint you so much with your brother's past. It's Camille, Camille Bisset...uh...his girl."

* * *

"Camille is a forty-two year old chick, born and bred in Quebec City, Canada," he began the story. "She was a figure-skater, winning many awards, but never made it onto the Olympic team. She heard that her brother had been a second-string quarterback for the Saskatchewan's Canadian football team. At eighteen she was offered a scholarship to Rutgers. She moved to the United States two months later and got citizenship. Half of her family lives in northern California, and her second cousin is the former mayor of Eureka, which made her attempt easy. She doesn't know her father, nor does she ever speak of him. She and her mother, Genevieve, are very close, however. Her mother has been retired from Smith's department store for six years now. She lives alone in Nova Scotia, in the same house her mother lived in and where Camille and her brother, Bradley, stayed most of each year," he explained.

"Camille graduated with honors four years later. She worked in sales and marketing for a large media firm in Philadelphia for years. She loved Philly with a passion until her rent got too high and her salary too low. She noticed an ad in a local rag for a teaching job down South—well, she got it," Hugo informed Francis. "It was teaching French at a private academy near the beach in Florida. She flew to Tampa, stayed on the campus, and had lots of students. She loved the position, but two years later, she was let go."

Francis, who had been listening attentively up to this point, butted in and asked, "She's no good at teachin', huh, Hugh?"

Hugo clarified, "No, she's very good. She speaks and knows French very well and loved the kids, you know, but there were massive budget cuts, and lots of the teachers were let go."

"So what happens next in the drama?" Francis asked Hugo.

Hugo followed with, "That's where you come in. It's all up to you. You see bud, Kenneth has dated her for about seven months now, and they know each other pretty well, inside and out. Twenty-six years separates them," Hugo said. "Kenneth is a mentor to her, since he's so smart. Camille loves intelligence, always did," Hugo said, smiling slyly and getting up out of the chair to get two Heinekens from the 'fridge. "Camille has a striking look about her," he went on. "She has long, straight, silver blonde hair with streaks of dark brown running throughout, which she parts down the center. She's tall, slim...has a boyish figure with no curves to speak of—except for her J-Lo butt," he chuckled. "She's classy as shit. I'm just telling you this so you know how to act around her," Hugo finished.

He told Francis to come and walk outside by the pool with him. When Hugo caught sight of the foreign orange-haired playmate wearing a pink, skin tight, v-neck t-shirt with shiny black low-rider hot pants and tall white boots, he impatiently snapped his fingers at her. She ran over to him. He placed two drink orders with her, while stroking her neck and back. She giggled. He smiled.

"You want me to impersonate Kenneth with Camille?" Francis asked in disbelief. "There's no way, Hugo. No way...can't do," Francis said with his eyes wide open.

"Francis, I have photos, tapes...bits of footage of their meetings at restaurants and bars, and even at her home and her school," Hugo confirmed. "Everything's mint. It'll be an Academy Award winning performance, but you have to be confident—otherwise, you're right," Hugo stressed, "there's no way it'll work. It's totally up to you.. The ball's in your court. And don't forget...."

Francis nervously broke in and asked, "Don't forget what?"

Hugo questioned him, "Remember I said there was a bonus for a job well done?"

Francis asked, "What cut of meat are you throwing to me?"

Hugo answered, "A prime cut. For a job well done, you will have more money than you've ever dreamed of. Again, you'll be Kenneth, in mind and money, with more broads than you've ever seen. Kenneth could get any woman on this planet, you know. Money buys the world, man. To be straight, you'll be taking in all his money, except for the split but we'll talk about that later when everything's said and done. Are you with us?" Hugo asked him.

Francis shrugged his shoulders, mouthed some words, and shook his head in disbelief. Seeing his reaction, Hugo flipped out and went into a tirade, punching his fist on the cabana wall. He screamed out, "Fran, don't fuck with us." Hearing all the commotion, the boys gathered quickly and mulled around the cabana, scoping out the situation. Francis was now angry; he felt disgraced and disrespected by Hugo.

* * *

Francis was given a brandy to settle his nerves and escorted to a huge bedroom that had an elegant four-poster bed and French doors which led to a jacuzzi bathroom with black marble tile throughout. The orange-haired playmate was waiting there for him, wearing only a chain around her hips. She led him over to the bed, stroking his private parts while tearing off his clothing. She laid her long orange hair over his entire genitalia. He tried to abstain but couldn't. He rolled her over, inserted his manhood in her, then squealed in ecstasy to his demons. A few seconds later, Francis was asleep, passed-out, and his playmate had absconded with Francis's five one hundred dollar bills in her hand.

When Francis awoke the next morning, he was dazed and confused. He didn't remember what had happened the previous night. Then he put on his trousers and noticed his money was gone from his pocket. Then he remembered everything. He realized he had to play this game with the mob in order to stay alive and to acquire his deserved fortune—and not lose everything he already had. He went downstairs, found Hugo at the breakfast table, and said, "I'll do it."

Hugo laughed and said, "I knew you would. Now about Camille...you'll love her, probably end up marrying her, if I don't first. And if you can, try to settle her down and stop her gibbering about her obsessive political beliefs." Hugo added, with a sly smile, "She talks a lot...probably too much for most men. She has strong beliefs about her party, which she acquired through her political science professor at Rutgers. He's a closet Socialist. Camille can have a bad attitude, but she's true to her cause. I know you told me you lean toward the right, and she leans toward the left, but if you both lean more inward, toward each other, you'll meet in the middle. You can't be stubborn because Camille already has a very stubborn side to her. You must play this out for us," Hugo stressed.

"Thanks, but no thanks," Francis replied.

"Oh, but there's more. Camille was married once, ten years ago, to a super sharp-looking Irish-Italian guy named Jamie McEntyre," Hugo revealed through police reports the boys got from a cop buddy on the take. "She kept her maiden name during the marriage. Jamie was tall and dark, with a good physique and chiseled facial features. He had wavy hair that swept over the right side of his forehead, like he put it that way on purpose. Jamie was suave and smooth, always saying the right thing at the right moment...a real con artist. He had one fetish, however, and that was hitting Camille, followed by plenty of rough sex. At first Jamie did this only once in a while. Camille would leave, come back, and the cycle would begin again. He beat her on a regular basis for the last three years of their marriage, smiling after each episode and going out to meet the world with wit and charm. Sometimes there was a period of weeks when Jamie showed no signs of misbehaving, being the perfect husband, but when restless Jamie got tired of playing this role, he started fighting with her again, calling her names. The slapping started next, followed by hitting her head on the bathroom walls."

"One night, about midnight," Hugo painfully informed him, "when Camille came home from a girl's night out, Jamie met her at the door with a smile and a hug. Once fully inside the door, however, he slammed it shut and carried her into their bedroom, where he beat her up, almost killed her. Jamie beat her in the dark for three hours, raped her, then held her in his arms all night long. He evidently slammed her face into the bedroom walls so many times that the walls had permanent streaks of maroonish red. They had to be repainted with a darker colored purple paint to hide any remnants of that insane night. Also, hospital reports state that Camille has permanent damage in the muscle of her left arm. She can't bend it past a certain point anymore because he slammed her chest and arms into the wood floor so many times. She was a mess."

Next, Hugo pulled out a photo of a pretty young lady, with a page boy hair cut, and said, "Are you ready for this?" Unsure what Hugo was talking about, Francis nodded, shifting his eyes, looking around the kitchen.

"There is one main character left in the story, and that is his only wife, Jane," Hugo went on to say, pointing to the photo as he rambled. "They have a fifteen year age difference. No kids. Kenneth met her near Portland, Maine, when he was in Boston on leave before his father died." Hugo said that Jane worked in a souvenir shop by the water, and when Ken walked in, Jane's heart seemed to stop beating, and he showed Francis a photo of their initial encounter. He went on to say that they were inseparable after this first date, until Ken could take no more of the straight life and began to carouse around town. "She overlooked this in the beginning," Hugo added, "so he asked her to marry him; however, it lasted less than three years. It seems he cared more about his career and his provocative social life, drinking...and yes, women, than he did about his wife." He whispered slightly, "She told her parents about this, and they ransacked Kenneth and Jane's mansion one night, trying to find evidence for a divorce settlement. Can you believe it, Fran?" Hugo asked. "They committed a crime in the law's eyes...breaking and entering. The police were called, attorneys were on the scene, and they were divorced one month later." He never saw or talked to Jane again. Hugo added, "You know, Kenneth was the one that started the proceedings. He knew everyone and could get anything done, quickly and easily."

After the marriage, Kenneth invested in real estate ventures in the Tampa Bay area, where he liked living so much. He even bought a house on the Gulf in Sarasota, which he quickly sold as property taxes that year skyrocketed. He moved northward to St. Petersburg, where he found the small city dignified and classy, yet laid back, just like him. He quickly made an offer on a hotel downtown, which the owners accepted. He turned it into a money-making enterprise, and he stayed there until the urge to buy a ranch hit him, years later.

Chapter Ten

Hugo took out the keys from one of his black Italian slack's front pockets. He asked Francis to take a spin with him in his Lamborghini. They drove through the countryside to the coastline parallel to Nantucket Island. Hugo was silent as they motored at close to two hundred miles per hour on narrow, winding lanes. Hugo had been on the circuit as an Indy driver once upon a time, so he handled the road extremely well, especially at top speeds. At first Francis was very nervous, clutching his seat belt tightly, but when he saw that Hugo was more than in control, he felt safe— pretty safe, anyway. Even when a pro is driving at top speeds, one never knows what fate may have in store. When they drove into the next small town, located about five minutes north of Hugo's house, Hugo slowed way down around the first curve and started conversing with Francis. He said that he had one more important piece, probably the most difficult piece in the puzzle, which he had to expose.

Francis said, "Okay, shoot it to me."

Hugo interjected, "Hey, are you hungry?"

Francis hesitantly shrugged and said, "A little."

"The best patty melts and fries with mayo are served up right over there," Hugo told him, pointing toward the water. They pulled into a diner named The Onion Grill and ordered two patty melts, fries, and coffee.

Hugo started his spiel. He said that Kenneth has been subpoenaed to the federal courthouse in Tampa to testify against an accused murderer who supposedly had a law degree and had passed the bar. This trial was to begin in eleven days.

Hugo lethargically went on as he sipped his hot coffee, which was just poured in his cup, and on the saucer, by their short, slim, grey-haired waitress. "Kenneth sometimes works the front desk of his city apartment complex when he's stayin' there." He said that the boys had a lot of sound and video recordings. "One day," he said, "A gentleman dressed as a construction worker and carrying a hard hat entered through the open doors of the apartment complex, came up to the desk, and asked, 'Are there any rooms for rent?' 'The sign out front says there are.' Kenneth answered. 'We've got whatever you need, one or two bedrooms, even a studio available for weekly or monthly rates.' The man answered, 'A studio is all I need, for a week at a time.' Kenneth stressed that rent is due on the first of every week. 'A one hundred dollar deposit is due, along with the first rental amount of one hundred fifty dollars,' he specified. 'No problem,' the renter said as he laid out three one hundred dollar bills on the counter. He added, 'Put the change on my account.'"

Hugo said the man was given the key after Kenneth xeroxed a copy of the renter's driver's license. The man's name was Donnie Crabtree. Hugo was careful to point out that Kenneth told the authorities he did not know much about the accused, what crimes he had committed in his past, or what was doing at present. Kenneth stressed to the police that Donnie was merely a tenant. Hugo stared at Francis like a teacher demeaningly stares at a pupil, and he slowly stated, "At the meeting with the state prosecutors, Francis, you must know the day and time their agreement was consummated and the amount of cash that was taken in, and these answers must glide gracefully off your tongue. The hotel is not providing us with bookkeeping records for every tenant, so, Francis, you're to retrieve these records before the questioning," Hugo sarcastically stated. He emphasized that copies needed to be made in case the prosecutors wanted to view them.

Francis finally got a word in edgewise and broke in with, "What did Donnie do, anyway?"

"A lot," answered Hugo. He continued, "He would call up numbers in the want ads, you know, people who were selling their cars. He'd arrange a time to meet 'em and drive the car. He would tell them he wanted to drive it in a wide open lot or field and see how it handled on rougher terrain. The individuals, or couples, would accompany him, and once away from civilization, Donnie would shoot them in the head and leave with the vehicle. By the way, the cars had to be imports. This was how he made his living. He would sell each car in the black market, pocket the money, and do it all over again. He's a sick mother-fucker," Hugo grimaced, "I don't know why he had to kill people just to steal cars. I think he enjoyed shooting people dead, with one shot in the mouth or between the eyes," Hugo continued, a sparkle in his eyes. "He got some fuckin' thrill from it.

Anyway, the defense is trying to blame the murders on a black man named Henry who's out on parole and who lived in the same building as Donnie. The black man's identification card was found next to the most current set of bodies in Tampa. The card probably fell out of the black man's pocket or was stolen by Donnie and placed by the bodies to pin it on Henry. Donnie has left a trail of these "want ad" killings from Texas to Florida and hasn't been convicted yet. With the prosecution team and state attorney having so much evidence and so many witnesses, Donnie should now be able to find his place in society, either in solitary confinement or on death row. You will be a key player in this trial, so don't blow it. Just listen to the tapes and watch the video clips 'til you get bored from repetition. You'll do fine. Just remember, you only have eleven days, and Fran...you've got to trace his signature and learn how to scribble it naturally. You never know when you'll have to sign somethin', especially the back of a check, y'know what I mean?" Hugo chuckled and gave Francis a wink.

After fifteen minutes, the sandwiches arrived at the wobbly table. Hugo asked for more coffee and "Red and yellow." Grey hair came bobbing out of the kitchen, holding a big coffee pot in one hand and two small jugs of mustard and ketchup in the other. A glob of homemade mayonnaise had already been placed inside each basket next to the fries for dipping, as was their signature. They both gobbled every morsel on their plates.

After about thirty minutes, the sun had just about set completely, and that meant the party at Hugo's home would soon fizzle out. Hugo and Francis sauntered out to Hugo's Lamborghini, where they found a gathering of people stationed around the car, admiring it. Hugo unlocked the doors with his key pad. "This is what you have to look forward to, Fran," Hugo slurred under his breath, his head held high. "This ain't too hard a life for ya, boy...is it?" He smugly asked as he climbed inside his toy. The race car peeled off in the direction of Logan Airport. It was now time to begin the drama.

Francis flew first class down to Tampa late that night, with Hugo by his side. They drank stiff gin and tonics that the pretty little Korean flight attendant continually presented to them. When one was half gone, she brought another, and another, then another. Finally she asked if they needed anything further as the jet descended. Hugo screeched loudly, in an obnoxious, drunken way, "Of course, sweetie! Where will you be after I get my bags?"

The attendant said, "I'll wait for you down at baggage claim."

"Okay," Hugo smiled. He knew he had scored.

At baggage claim, the Korean girl was waiting for Hugo, who had stopped into an airport bar to get a beer, with a more sober Francis. When Hugo finally arrived downstairs, drunk, the carousel had stopped spewing out baggage but the Korean was still waiting there, patiently and submissively. Francis took control at that point and went into the baggage claim office, where the female working behind the counter pointed to two bags and officially said, "Are these two yours? They were just brought in. If they are, you need to show me some identification before you can leave with them." He showed his I.D., picked up his sports bag, then went back to get Hugo's I.D. Walking back slowly, he looked around the claim area curiously. It was empty of people. There was no one in sight. Hugo was gone.

Francis signed for a non-descript sports utility vehicle at the heavily occupied lot on the fourth level, and he sped off to the ranch, not knowing when or where he was to meet up with Hugo again.

On the interstate, he called Hugo for instructions. Hugo answered and asked, "Are you there yet?" "Just about," Francis dryly answered as he heard giggles in the background.

"Get him," Hugo ordered as he pushed the end button on his cell.

Hugo was clearly "busy," Francis surmised as he sped toward the motel in Bradenton.

Chapter Eleven

The cool Halloween wind was howling with frightening yells and the unlatched windows were banging when Francis regained consciousness a few hours later. He felt the back of his knotted, bloody skull. His hand felt wet when he rubbed his head and neck; both were soaked in blood. He wondered to himself, trying to remember what had happened, *What could have caused this?* He would soon find out as he looked around the now littered sitting room.

One open window was coming off its hinges with the strong, blustery wind gusts that barged their way inside the bedroom and swirled the foliage lying on the carpet around the room. Francis strategically raised his body off the floor as he stretched out a hand and grabbed a nearby chair for support. When he finally got vertical, Francis saw the huge pieces of branch which evidently were the cause of his head injury. They were laying throughout the sitting area, splaying the couch and chairs with dirt and holes. He looked over and saw Kenneth, still sound asleep, unbelievably, having had such a sudden, violent storm in his room. Francis breathed a huge sigh of relief, when he saw the almost emptied crystal brandy snifter sitting beside the bed. He then knew why Kenneth was sleeping so soundly.

Francis knew he had to execute this plan before the break of day, which seemed about to enter the room and say hello at any moment. Francis replaced the pink baby aspirin in the aspirin bottle, which Kenneth took once a day, with mild-dosed arsenic pills. He then pulled out the stun gun the boys gave him and shot it into Kenneth's lean thigh. He forced the first set of sedatives through his twin's wind pipes, then pushed the needle, which was only a quarter filled with a very mild dose of arsenic, into Kenneth's derriere. Next he pulled Kenneth off the bed. He dragged him into the large walk-in closet, which was filled with all types of military garb. Francis gagged Kenneth with one of the many bandanas found on the shelf. He stuffed the cloth inside his mouth and tied another around his head, over Kenneth's eyes. Then Francis sloppily dragged Kenneth down the hallway and down each one of the tall, specially crafted steps. At the bottom of the staircase was the large mahogany-floored entry. Francis had to be particularly careful not to slip on the highly polished real wood floor while holding Kenneth. He knew he had to place Kenneth in the rental before the girls started their daily duties.

He put a black tarp over Kenneth's body and dragged him to the utility vehicle. This way it appeared that Kenneth was perhaps a piece of machinery that needed some attention at a nearby repair shop. Francis shoved Kenneth inside, leaving his legs bent and arms dangling under the tarp that was placed on top of the back seat. His first acting scene of the drama seemed about to begin as he glanced up, while climbing into the driver's seat, and noticed Gimpie's sparkling midnight blue Dodge Caravan coming down the estate's gravel roadway. It appeared to be several years old but still in mint condition. Francis revved up his engine, locked the doors, let down his window, and his guard, and began his spontaneous script.

"Hey, Gimpie. Glad you could join us today," Francis yelled out to the driver of the Caravan. Gimpie boldly pointed out that she was fifteen minutes early. Those two had had a running feud for years, which Francis played to the hilt. With two and a half weeks of watching his twin socialize, through photos and from afar through binoculars, he knew all of the correct moves to fit each mood of Kenneth's personality. With the microscopic bugging chip placed between one of the links on Kenneth's watch, which Kenneth wore religiously, Francis perpetually knew the right words to say in any given situation, along with the exact sounds of speech to make, which mimicked Kenneth's vocal patterns.

As Francis pulled out of the ranch and headed up the interstate toward Hugo's estate in Massachusetts, Gimpie screamed to him, "Hey, what's with the new Chevy?"

Francis shouted back, "Its a rental. I've got a long sales trip ahead of me. Didn't want to put the mileage on my Cadillac, Gimp."

She nodded, smiling in approval as good business managers do when their boss has made a practical decision on his or her own. He knew driving to Massachusetts would be a long, hard ride, so he decided to take the more direct route and go up Ninety-five the whole way, after taking Interstate Four to Orlando.

Hugo's basement was the decisive location for keeping Kenneth until they completed poisoning him, because it had such spacious living quarters. It was a very comfortable spot for the procedure to take place. Here, Dr. Martin's injections for Kenneth's demise could be administered without any interference.

Francis got a call on the car phone before he reached the interstate. He felt hesitant to answer it when he saw the name flashing, "Cassie Cay." Remembering all of the race horses he recently sold to her over the phone, and what she was going to pay for each, he took the call. Sounding short on time, just as his brother would have, he agreed to meet Cassie at her home in Ocala that afternoon to discuss the sale of one of his favorite and most promising colts. He promised to bring her race horses with him in the trailer as well. Francis turned around on the two-lane highway several minutes from his property, which led to the interstate, and forged back to the ranch to hook up his trailer and load it with "pieces of gold."

* * *

Hugo was at the end of the drive, waiting on Francis, two days later. When the Chevy turned into the pebbled driveway, Hugo told Francis to park near the basement entrance in back. There was no one on the property except for Doc Martin, who was standing at the back door, holding a big black medical supply bag.

Francis wearily parked, Hugo came running up behind, and Martin gently maneuvered Kenneth out of the vehicle and into the house. The doc dragged Kenneth down the basement stairs with the help of

Francis. Hugo was on the phone with one of the boys as he scoped the situation outside.

When Kenneth was laid out on the bed downstairs, Doc Martin told Francis he was going to inject his twin with penicillin and a "trifle of arsenic" every day for several weeks, a little at a time, until he "pops off." Martin explained to Francis, and Hugo, who had just come downstairs, that over a period like this, it seemed plausible to die from simply an allergic reaction to penicillin. The autopsy would probably not show the miniscule amounts of arsenic administered to Kenneth on a daily basis, causing a slow, undetectable, poison-filled death. "Francis, you really are allergic to penicillin, so Kenneth, who has become Francis, unknowingly, must be allergic to penicillin too. Francis Cranford will die from injections given by a young, incompetent candy-striper, who, by the way, is scheduled to arrive here at any minute. She will be his live-in caretaker."

Breaking in and taking over the story, Hugo continued, "Doc will put penicillin in the bottles marked codeine, and you can guess what happens after that." Hugo ended up by saying, "Start being Kenneth right now, in your body and in your soul, 'cause you've got lots of things to do and places to be, as Kenneth, and you know, he'll be dead in a few short weeks."

Francis asked Hugo, "Why does he supposedly need pain pills, anyway, Hugh?"

Martin dryly answered, "Because he has just had his birthmark, under his left eye, removed by me. Remember, he's you and you're him."

Francis continued the questioning, "What's going to happen to the nurse who ends up killing him?" Hugo shrugged his right shoulder, lifting it high, saying nothing. Francis felt another tinge of sensitivity but quickly dismissed it when Hugo placed a five hundred dollar bill in his black polo shirt pocket, one of the many polos that now made up the bulk of his new wardrobe.

As he looked at Hugo and said, "What the fuck is...?" The heavy door slammed above the staircase and a young, walleyed, freckle-faced redhead came trotting down the stairs, singing, "Sorry 'm late.... Gut cuot 'n trafk."

Francis looked at Hugo in disbelief.

"Yes, she is slightly retarded," Hugo murmured pitifully. "Oh well."

* * *

Francis went ahead and brought the colt with the other two race horses over to Cassie's home the afternoon he began the drive to Hugo's. He ate a late breakfast at a run-down diner in the area, where he was served burnt bacon and toast. The coffee was okay, but nothing like his own. He greeted the cosmetic queen with a hug, as he had seen the two embracing in Kenneth's photos, and he very animatedly spoke to the woman, not sounding short on time now. No, now he was patiently awaiting a big, fat check in exchange for the thoroughbred horses he was about to unveil and the promising colt.

Of course, she had to have the colt when she laid her eyes on it. She reached in her designer handbag and pulled out a wad of cash, handing it to him, and she gave him a peck on the cheek. "This should be more than enough," she chanted. "Count it now."

He turned away from her, as he had seen Kenneth do on many occasions, and shook his head, "No."

81

After about an hour of flirtatious chit-chat about the weather, the economy, and what-not, Francis left Cassie Cay's property with cash in hand. He drove to one of Kenneth's banks in Ocala, deposited half, and kept half. All of Kenneth's horse sales were done on strictly a cash basis. He provided the client with a better price, not having a paper trail, and of course, he reaped the benefits this way and could stash these benefits right in his jean pockets.

Francis traveled across Florida selling horses and colts to wealthy names and addresses. His black angus cattle was sold to popular grocery store chains. Francis now felt he was going to accrue tens of thousands for himself, just from his brother's ranch business, and in just a matter of weeks. There was to be a split, however. The mob would more than likely receive tens of thousands in profits from the citrus growing business, in a short period of time, and each agreed to run one of the two enterprises completely and solely by themselves, so as to avoid disagreements and stalemates.

* * *

The mob had a horrible grudge against Kenneth. Kenneth was supposed to give the boys half of all profits from the ranch and estate for the first five years and one-third from then on. Kenneth didn't hold his part of the bargain—hence the slow, painful payback. He had paid principal and interest on the property for only a couple of years. Then he stopped, hoarding all the money. After thirteen years, the Irish boys decided to finally get back all the principal and interest loaned for start-up costs on the multi-million dollar enterprise, plus more, a lot more. When their scheme was to fully unravel, the boys were to make millions through the life insurance policy, but more importantly, through the five thousand acres of citrus groves producing citrus products for shipment throughout the country, all year long, with costly prices attached to them.

Francis had sole rights to the horse and cattle business, only because he was the one who knew about these animals. The boys knew nothing about this business venture and didn't want to be bothered with "pets," as they referred to them. With his newly acquired evil attitude, Francis did extremely well in his business, even better than his brother had. Now he was finally able to live the life of which he'd always dreamed.

Chapter Twelve

Dreaming of his favorite submarine sandwich, consisting of crab meat stacked high and thinly-sliced swiss and provolone cheeses placed on a crisp, seasoned Italian roll and topped off with Francis' secret spicy butter and mayo sauce, a char-grilled onion, and three tomato slices, Francis slept soundly, unaware of his radio alarm clock playing "fifties" music for close to half an hour. He was finally awakened by the ringing of the telephone on the nightstand next to his bed. "Yeah," he muttered as he coughed.

The voice on the other end yelled, "Asshole, wake up, or you're gonna blow everything."

Francis jumped out of bed, recognizing Hugo's voice, looked at the clock, then hung up the phone, saying nothing to Hugo. Francis was in a panic, as he realized that he only had an hour to get dressed, eat something, and drive all the way to downtown Tampa. "Sh-sh-shit!" he stuttered as he squeezed into his faded Wranglers and cowboy boots. He grabbled one of the tight black muscle shirts hanging in his closet and slung it over his rugged shoulders. He splashed cold water on his face, brushed his teeth and hair, grabbed a stale bagel from the bag on the dusty motel dresser, and flew out the door.

Francis had flown in with Hugo the night before. Francis didn't realize the air-conditioning in his Escalade needed coolant since he hadn't driven it for a while. He turned off its unit completely. He was miserable and began to sweat profusely.

He sped along the city interstate until he reached the tall, massive federal courthouse. He parked in one of the few lots that still had space, got out, and sprinted into the building. He was soaked in sweat at this point, and fifteen minutes late.

When he ran from the elevator into the lobby, outside of the trial room, he was greeted by a displeased Hugo. Hugo said something that Francis did not understand, and he pushed Francis inside. It seems that they had just called Francis to testify, and Hugo told the bailiff that "Mr. Redman" would be arriving momentarily, which, thankfully, he did...for Francis's sake.

Francis held his own in the trial. He did a superb job of reciting the facts of his several short conversations with the accused, and of course, he had paperwork and dates and times of contract signings and payments received from Donnie. He had managed to confiscate all the needed files and receipt books from the locked back office at the apartment building. He had picked the lock. Hugo brilliantly had showed him how. The prosecutor had Francis on the stand for only about twenty minutes as his testimony hurt the defense, due to contradictory statements made by Francis.

When the defense attorney, who was tough as nails and able to bring anyone down in the witness box, let Francis step down after only two of his questions, Hugo felt relieved. "Sorry, bud," Hugo humbly told him as he wrinkled his forehead. "You did *magnifique!*" Hugo patted him hard on the back, saying that there should be no more hassle with the authorities about this situation. Hugo felt that the jury would find him guilty and give Donnie life in prison, or death, for sure.

The next morning the verdict was in, and it proved to be the latter.

* * *

Before Francis was to drive back to Boston, he had to go over the previous month's accounting records with Sciara and McCarty. This was done like clockwork on the first Monday of each month. He drove over to the apartment complex and entered through the same back door he had used to confiscate the needed records for the trial.

Francis strolled into the lobby wearing a white Izod t-shirt, blue shorts, and sandals with socks. This was Kenneth's daily attire. He had gotten used to wearing socks with sandals from his days in Germany. He enjoyed not having his feet perspire this way.

Francis walked down the hall to the building's hidden office and opened the large frame of the big black door by its shiny brass knob, which hung a little too low. He cheerfully acknowledged the two men with, "Hey, guys, yous ready to do it?"

Pete frowned and said, "We've got to."

In two hours they completed their project and went to the bar up the street, like they always did. Blaine came shuffling through the entrance, laughing, "Hey, studs, what's up?" He told the fat bar maid to pour him a draft and a Schnapps, which he always drank together. After a few more rounds, and conversations with scantily-clad women, Blaine was sufficiently hammered and couldn't walk back to his apartment. Francis offered to take him home. Blaine accepted and fell down, head first. The bouncer came to his rescue, picked Blaine off the floor, and placed him vertically on solid ground.

The drive up the road to Blaine's proved disastrous. Francis did not know exactly where his place was and couldn't ask him for help, as he was passed out in the back seat. He had to call Hugo. Hugo gave him the address. It was only two minutes up the road, and Francis stayed in the Escalade with him until the booze wore off. After fifteen minutes, Blaine awoke and walked upstairs, by himself, into his abode.

* * *

"It's now time," Hugo told Francis. "Kenneth should be out of his misery in about one more week."

Martin said that Kenneth was like a vegetable, unable to speak or move. He was in a virtual coma. "Anyway," he assured the two, "It won't be too much longer."

In the basement, Kenneth was completely incapacitated, just lying there, staring at the ceiling. Francis got one last twinge of guilt as he looked into Kenneth's lifeless eyes, which he was sure once gleamed and glowed with delight and passion. Hugo moved his own hands up and down, as if to break Francis out of the trance he was in, and it worked. Still in a state of thought, Francis watered-up the syringe, and had the so-called nurse place the needle in Kenneth's left hand, where the veins were strong and sturdy.

Francis, Hugo, and the retarded girl continued with this procedure on a daily basis for six days. Every day Kenneth became more and more like a vegetable, having very little ability to move any part of his body. On the seventh day, Kenneth awoke with a startle, his eyes wide open, but didn't have any feeling, anywhere; then he simply closed his eyes with a snorting moan.

The candy-striper went into Kenneth's room with a tray of injections. While trotting down the narrow staircase to administer this new dose to Kenneth, Hugo and Francis heard a blood-curdling scream. They were my by a hysterical young waif in a candy-stripers uniform. She grabbed the two, each by one arm, and pulled them over to the bed. She screamed, "Uh, m gud, whut di'I du?" Then she burst into tears and screeched, "N' pulz! He deaad!"

The retarded candy-striper hadn't understood why Kenneth wasn't improving, only getting worse, and she could not defend herself against accusations made by Hugo. The detectives were called, handcuffs were placed on the girl, and a determination by the courts was made that the curly redhead was to be held with no bail on charges of first-degree murder.

Chapter Thirteen

There was no funeral. The mob boys simply dug out ground in the back of Hugo's grandiose estate and plopped the body down deep inside. They covered the now filled hole with dirt and wedged a wood branch in the top so that they would remember its location.

Not many people really knew him, so the supposed death of Francis did not really effect anyone. In his personal and business life, Francis kept very close to himself, letting few inside his realm.

Getting greedier and greedier with time and events, the real Francis now wanted to sell Kenneth's estate and pocket all the earnings. He was getting so clever and so bold he didn't even care about cheating the almighty Irish mobsters. He felt a little nervous at this prospect but said to himself, "Oh, what the hell. This life's no good without it, without lots of the green shit, so I'll take the risk and even consider it fun."

Three days after Kenneth's death, Viola Hopkins was charged with second-degree murder and sentenced to life in an insane asylum. Her retardation was the key factor in this determination. The jury thought her to be schizophrenic, needing to be monitored twenty-four/seven.

On the news later that night, Francis saw the nurse sobbing hysterically, but he didn't get any twinge of sorrow or guilt. The twinges were gone. He had no more sympathy left in him. Now he was completely in the hands of Satan, administering the devil's wishes to whomever and whatever.

* * *

Francis contacted two developers who had left their cards tucked in the electronic gate several days earlier. The first one offered five million; the second one offered six. He met the second developing firm to complete the deal that evening. It was now done. Francis had scammed the mob. He had become very brazen, but knew he still had to be wary and careful of everybody and everything.

Francis called Doc Martin and requested his help. He told him he would pay him one million dollars to fake Mr. Redman's death. Since Kenneth was a closet chain smoker, Francis thought it fitting that he die of lung cancer which was diagnosed too late. Worshiping money, the doc smiled from ear to ear and jumped at his proposal. He also wasn't worried about going against the mob.

The next morning Martin got "Mr. Redman" admitted to the Veteran's Hospital near Clearwater. Having a PET scan done, Martin determined that it was inoperable cancer, too far gone, and proceeded to transfer him to the hospice unit. The news crews were all over this story.

Hugo called the doc in hysteria. The doc told him it was true. "Francis has lung cancer. He sure didn't seem sick when we all first met him up in Boston. He seemed just fit and trim, but its almost all over for him. When he's dead I'll arrange to have him placed in a fancy casket and then flown to Arlington. I'll call the State Department to notify them of these plans," Doc Martin advised Hugo.

"Well, that's good news for us. Now we don't have to whack him, and we already have the insurance money and citrus contracts. We just need to either sell the estate for a massive profit or learn the 'pet' business," Hugo belted out, smirking.

When Camille found out Kenneth was dying of lung cancer, after reading a blurb in the *St. Petersburg Times*, she drove to the Veteran's Hospital to see him at once. When she arrived, however, she was told that no one was permitted to see him. Camille raised her deep voice one octave and said, "But I'm his girlfriend. Doesn't that matter?"

The nurse, who was escorted down the hallway by Doc Martin, said, "You must leave."

Camille stormed out, shaking her long streaked hair. She had no idea what she had done wrong. "Why is he so damn mad at me? What did I do? Jáime Kenny Beaucoup, *mere. Cést que ce?* She called her mother in Quebec to ask.

The following day Camille drove to the hospital, where she marched straight upstairs to Kenneth's private room. Getting ready for a major battle with the nursing staff, she breathed deeply several times, in and out. As she approached the nurse's station, she heard, "Oh my God," followed by quick, heavy footsteps running down the hall. "In here. There's no heartbeat. Let's pump it out."

Camille burst into the Kenneth's shut-tight room, panic stricken. Doc Martin put his arm around her and, looking at the ground, said, "Kenneth's dead." Camille was devastated.

She ran over to a tranquilized Francis and kissed him on the lips, whispering, "*Mon ami*," into his ear. Then she demeaningly said to Martin, as she opened Kenneth's mouth to pull out his dentures, "Don't you and your crew know how to do your job? These, "putting her hands on his teeth," should have been taken out immediately." Camille ranted, raved, and harped, "You inadequate, incompetent retards! His teeth were knocked out years ago in the war. You should have known that." Reaching her boiling point, she grabbed his teeth and tried to pull his dentures out. She tried and tried but was unable.

Perplexed, she stared at his stained but sturdy teeth and looked up wild-eyed at Doc Martin and said, "That's not him, not Kenny."

Doc Martin shot her with a heavy dose of morpheme. It took thirty seconds until she went to sleep. The doc then left the hospital by taxi, never to return, with a one million dollar check, dated a week earlier, on his person—his destination: Mexico, by way of Boston.

The doc had to retrieve his belongings from his high-rise apartment. He was scheduled to fly to Cabo San Lucas the next evening, where he was to purchase a beachfront mansion equipped with a staff of servants. At a convenience store payphone along the way, the doc left Hugo a belittling message on his cell, "I outsmarted you, you dimwit."

After this episode, Francis knew he must also leave the country, leave the continent for that matter, and quickly. He disguised himself, sneaked out of the hospital, and flew the Lear jet to Atlanta Municipal. From there he took a taxi to Hartsfield and caught a DC-10 non-stop to Lucerne, then on to Athens. Using his twin's credentials, he was able to get into Switzerland and Greece without waiting in either country's airports' tremendously long customs line. Once out of the airport in Athens, Francis was whisked off to the seaport, in a long black sedan, to where the island ferries were docked.

Francis had to wait in the blinding sun for close to an hour until the ship was ready for boarding. He carried his one bag with him onboard. He only brought with him three pairs of jeans, one pair of shorts, and five shirts. His clothes horse days appeared to be over, even though he had over five hundred million dollars in his Swiss bank account and could buy anything he had ever wanted. Francis had had this money transferred from Tampa to Die Welt, a reputable Swiss bank in Lucerne. When he arrived at this neutral country's financial institution, it was there that he also added another authorized user to this new account, Irwin Stuart, his alias.

Walking out of the revolving doors of the tall, impressive bank, Die Welt, onto the sidewalk filled with fast-paced, business-attired pedestrians, Francis accidentally bumped into a non-yielding, fair-skinned and haired man who spoke with an Irish accent. "Sorry, chap," the young freckle-faced man apologizingly spoke.

"Oh, no. It's my fault," Francis sarcastically mocked, and he flagged down a taxi for the airport.

Chapter Fourteen

Upon Francis a.k.a. Kenneth's death, the "Irish clan" was to receive his property. Francis knew this, that they were playing him, because this clause had already been drawn up by the mob lawyers, in small print, at the bottom of the contract between the two parties. Francis had read this with a magnifying glass the night after the signing.

"You guys are never gonna see any of it," was the undistinguishable, strange sounding message left on Hugo's machine. This message was left for Hugo the morning Francis departed for Greece. Hugo heard it but didn't bother with it. He thought it to be simply a prank.

Feeling angry, confused, emotional, and dumbfounded, yet delighted at this twist of fate, Hugo contacted the mob's law firm. He spoke to the big, burly Chicago attorney about these unforeseen circumstances. Attorney Gambino said he would handle everything. "I'm gonna tie everything up in a pretty package for you guys. I'll get back with you after I make some calls," Gambino quietly said. "And for all the presents you sent my sick girl, this one's on the house." Gambino's eleven-year old had been diagnosed with acute lymphoma two months earlier and was going through intense treatments. Her chances for survival were 50 percent. The boys sent her elaborate doll houses and toy stoves and ovens, along with rare antique dolls. Alison received these presents every week, after each treatment. They made her so happy she forgot everything she had just gone through. Gambino was very appreciative, to say the least.

Hugo fell asleep on his recliner waiting on the call from Gambino. When he opened his eyes, he saw on his cell, which had mistakenly been on silent the entire time, that he had two missed calls and two urgent messages. One was from Gambino and the other from an unknown caller, so he hurriedly put in his secret code on the land line to retrieve the messages. He placed them on speaker and first heard, "Got real bad news, Hugh. Are ya sitting down?"

Hugo said to himself, "No, but I will be...shoot."

Gambino started the scenario, "Well, Hugh, it seems that Francis sold the entire estate, horses, cattle, oranges, grapefruits...everything. He pocketed all of the change before he died. We don't know where it's stashed. It'll take some time, but we'll find out. But, Hugh, now we're gonna have to bill you."

Hugo solemnly told Gambino upon calling him, "I understand," and continued, "Why would he hide the money in a different account than Kenneth's anyway? He has been using that vault for over a month. They all know 'im there and think he's Kenneth. It was peachy, so why did he do this?"

"Don't know, but we'll find out real soon," Gambino assured. "Gotta go, I'll talk to ya soon." Then there was a dial tone.

The second urgent message was from an unknown number but had a very recognizable voice from the immediate past. It was Doc Martin. The doc boldly raved, "We snowed you, bro. You are never gonna see any of it. You're history, so you better start packing, 'cause you're going down. Too bad you can never find me now." Then there was a click, followed by a dial tone.

Mad as a bull, Hugo raced his rented silver Porsche down the interstate from the five-star hotel in Sarasota to the Parrish exit ramp, near Bradenton. He slowed down when he got on the two-lane road that fronted the evil five thousand acres. He came to a halt when he found Jude and Gimpie in the road, flagging down traffic. It seemed one of the ranch hands had had a heart attack when he heard Kenneth perished.

The girls had called 911, but it had already taken ten minutes and they were worried about permanent brain damage if he did not get medical attention, fast. Sirens blasted through the air, along with screeching brakes, as the ambulance encountered Hugo's Porsche parked in the middle of the road.

The paramedics brought out the stretcher and ran over to where Emilio was, on the other side of the iron gate, with his own pony staring down at him. They said Emilio was semi-conscious. They evidently got to him just in time. The paramedics loaded Emilio onto the ambulance and noisily sped off.

The two girls asked Hugo to come inside for a drink as an offering of thanks, which he gladly accepted. He told the girls how sorry he was to hear of their tragedy.

Gimpie said, "He's already sold the ranch, and I don't know where I'm goin' now." She cried, "I liked it so much here."

Jude added, "Well, I know where I'm scheduled to be in one hour...at my clinic in Pinellas Park. Wish I could have met you under better circumstances, but life must go on." Jude sighed in a carefree manner and waved goodbye.

Leaving the residence herself, Gimpie told Hugo Jude would be fine because she had a thriving veterinary practice in Pinellas County. "She's always been so independent. She can survive anything, keeping a smile on her spirited face," Gimpie described Jude.

At that moment Kimmie came barging through the door in hysterics. "I can't believe he's dead. I was just talking to him last week and he seemed fine, a little out of it. He didn't remember my most favorite birthday when he gave me a miniature pony, but I just chalked that up to age. I'm so sorry this happened...I hate that stupid doctor. How could he not have known about the cancer before?

"It was apparently diagnosed too late, the news said," Hugo replied.

"How did that doctor ever get his medical license?" Kimmie blurted out. "Kenneth always got an annual physical. How could this quack have not seen any signs then?"

Hugo replied, "Maybe it happened that fast. They say you never know."

At that moment, Kimmie fainted.

"Let me go to the ranch infirmary and get some smelling salts for her. I'll be right back," Gimpy said, running out.

Hugo went out to his car, reached in his carryall, and opened the chloroform, drenching the white cloth napkin he also had pulled out of the bag. Hugo met

Gimpie at the back door when she returned with the salts and grabbed her from behind, pushing the drenched napkin onto her face until she passed out and fell onto the tiled floor, then he gave her a boatload of sleeping pills to make sure she was knocked out for a good while.

Hugo picked her up and placed her on the couch where had been sitting earlier and proceeded to look around the property. He ransacked all of the drawers, file cabinets, and entertainment centers, but he found nothing...no information. He began to walk to the tool shed located way in the back of the rectangularly-shaped estate when he noticed the Lear jet was gone. He thought this to be very odd and called Gambino immediately. Hugo found out the lear jet was not reported as stolen. "There's more to this story," Hugo blurted out to the cattle standing beside him.

Hugo stayed the night in the barn behind the house, thinking about what must happen next in the scheme. At seven in the morning he was awakened by a long-axialed cattle truck whose driver was herding the last of the cows, it seemed, into his "barn on wheels." Hugo went outside and, acting like a ranch hand, he asked him who he was picking up for.

The driver said, "My bills say Cannon Meat Processors."

The cattle was all gone, probably sold to processing plants and grocery store chains. There were no thoroughbreds in sight, either. Hugo thought, *Francis must have sold all fifteen to Cassie and the rest of his millionaire clientele before he died—or skipped town,* as he now was beginning to believe.

* * *

Hugo had no other choice but to call Camille. He looked up her cell records to get the number. She answered in her usual deep but perky French-accented voice, "Haello."

Hugo stated, "You don't know me, you've never seen me, but I've seen you, a lot."

She didn't say a thing.

Hugo continued, "Please, don't hang up. This is not a crank. I've got to talk to you about Kenneth, uuh...."

She immediately came to attention and quickly interrupted. "Well, I was supposed to catch a cheap flight late tonight to Washington for the funeral tomorrow. So...."

"How 'bout this evening?" he asked, interrupting her. "At the Gulfport marina. I'll rent a boat and bring some wine coolers, okay? Oh...how's about six?"

By seven they were both officially intoxicated. The boat was bobbing up and down as it was tied alongside the walkway of the pier. Here, Camille listened to Hugo's hour-long confession. It was not 100 percent accurate, however—not even 50 percent. Hugo was a master bull shitter and always had been. He reported that Francis and Kenneth had each taken over the other's persona for some money scheme. Francis died, and now Kenneth was dead, too.

Camille was astonished. She didn't even know Kenneth had a twin brother. That's why she drank more and more, not believing what she was listening to. She was almost in a state of shock.

* * *

It was unusually mild for an early December morning in D.C. Arlington National Cemetery was overflowing with people, all friends of Kenneth. The mob boys did not attend, so as not to bring attention to themselves. Camille was there, dressed to the hilt in black leather bought in Calgary. She and Hugo had caught a red-eye after their encounter at the pier. Hugo rested at the hotel, and a limo was waiting to carry her back there after the ceremony.

When the famed long-time senator from Massachusetts got on the podium to make his eulogy to Kenneth before the burial was set to take place, the crowd went silent. Kenneth and Senator Kenard went back a long way. They disagreed with each other's political views, hated each other's values, and put each other down in record time on every occasion. This happened on a perpetual basis, especially when they met at the American Legion building, near Beacon Hill, for drinks.

The senator started and ended his elegant tribute with applause. He stepped down and hugged Camille, who was standing beneath the podium. Half of the time Camille shed crocodile tears, and the other half real tears. She still wanted to know where the real Kenneth was. She thought perhaps he was still alive.

Camille climbed into the black limousine, lifting her long black leather skirt slightly so she didn't trip on it with her high heels. They motored to Hugo's hotel, up Interstate Ninety-five. The limo arrived at Hugo's hotel an hour later. Hugo greeted her with a hug and showed her to his bedroom. Camille was in a state of disarray as she told him she knew it wasn't really Kenneth.

Chapter Fifteen

Camille wasn't ready for what was to happen next. Hugo ripped off her blouse and said, "This is what you've been waiting for, isn't it?"

Camille fought and finally managed to pull away from him. He struggled to apologize, realizing how this impulsive flirtation could have ruined his whole plan.

Camille caught her breath, looked disgustedly at Hugo, and said, "I trusted you, for some reason."

Hugo defended his actions by sheepishly muttering, while on his knees, "You're just so pretty. I couldn't help myself. Please forgive me."

Hearing this, Camille felt a motherly instinct to nurture Hugo. She almost felt sorry for her words but still wanted to mend his ways. "It's all right," Camille said to him meekly as she sat on the fluffy ottoman. "Let's forget this ever happened and try to find Kenneth, okay?" she asked.

Hugo nodded and stood up. He got a Heineken from the mini refrigerator, popped the top, and planted a sweet one on her naturally plump, pink lips. "Tomorrow we start our plan of attack so we can complete this jigsaw," he boldly stated, pointing to the table across the room, where he had started his own puzzle of a Monet painting.

* * *

Hugo slept on the recliner, Camille in his bed. They were both exhausted from the horrendous flight late the night before when the jet was bombarded with golf ball sized hail as it put down its landing gear.

"Too much traveling!" Camille advised.

A thought provoked Hugo, "It takes the fun out of it when everything's on such a time schedule."

When morning came, they each took turns getting ready in the huge bathroom. Next they ordered room service. After eating corned beef hash and poached eggs, one of Hugo's favorite breakfasts, they took their strong black coffees with them. They climbed into Hugo's rental, which he signed for and picked up at the stand downstairs. This time the only foreign car available for rental was a convertible Jag. He thought Camille would probably like it, so he took it.

Hugo didn't know what was happening to him. All he could do was look at and think about this perfect girl with her straight, yard-long, silver and mocha streaked hair, wearing her tight jeans and worn out Rutgers rugby shirt with the sweet smell of baby powder all over it. Her thong sandals, which showed off French manicured toenails, really turned him on. This was his type of woman.

* * *

The sun was shining, but the wind was gusting as they made their way down to Arlington. The boys met the couple there, shovels in hands. They had paid off cemetery guards to look the other way as they exhumed the body. Digging for what seemed to be an hour, the boys finally reached the ornate casket. Pulling it up slowly with four shovels underneath, the boys sweated and cursed. Taking off their jackets, they showed four muscular young physiques through skin-tight, long-sleeved black shirts and "painted on" black jeans. They pried the casket open and lifted it hesitantly, not knowing what they might, or might not, find.

A puff of dust escaped from the empty coffin, which acted as a vacuum. Camille and the boys simply stared at one another in disbelief.

Hugo, frothing at the mouth, screamed, "Ohhhh... you are really gonna pay, Fran!" He ran to the Jag, got inside, and peeled off.

Camille sat on the resealed the coffin and cried.

A little while later, the boys put the hollow coffin back in the ground, leaving the mounds of dug-up dirt stationary, and gave Camille a ride to Hugo's hotel. She stayed there alone, all night, as a recluse. She put on footie pajamas and drank hot chocolate as she watched classic movies, crying. Hugo never called.

As the early morning sun glared at Camille through the balcony window, she awakened from her restless sleep. The irritating melody of her cell phone began to ring. "Haolo," she answered, her eyes still shut.

"Camille? This is Doc Martin. Remember me? I was the one who pronounced Kenneth dead at the VA."

"Yes, I remember you," she spoke softly. "How can I help you?"

"I've got secrets to tell...big ones," he revealed. "I was supposed to get a big fat sum for my services. Instead I got a big fat check from a closed bank account in Tampa. So I'm ready to spill the beans, but I want to tell you in person, not over the phone. I'll have tickets waiting for you at Dulles for the five o'clock flight on American to TPA. When you arrive in Tampa, a brown Hummer will pick you up at the arrival terminal. Come to a small two-seater in the back corner of the café on the first floor of Memorial Hospital. I'll be there with bells on." After catching his breath, Doc warned, "And remember, it's in your best interest to come alone."

Thirty minutes later, Camille heard Hugo outside the room, "Honey, are you still there?" He unlocked the door and stepped inside. With a blank stare, Camille grabbed his toned arm and pulled him close to her. She hugged him tightly and took off her faded rugby shirt and his musty-smelling gray turtleneck, rubbing her firm breasts on his erect nipples. He laid her down on the leather recliner and had his way with her. The two fell asleep soon after their ecstasy, primarily due to exhaustion. It had been a harrowing few days for everyone involved, with lies and schemes and set-ups which were all designed, in the end, to set Francis free, Francis and his millions.

* * *

Over lunch in a cozy Italian bistro on "K" street, near the air ticket shops, Camille couldn't wait to tell Hugo about the call she had just received from Doc Martin. He seemed more than interested to hear about this call. She told him, "The doc said he was supposed to get money from Kenneth if he said Kenneth died. Kenneth never paid him. It doesn't make sense to me, but he said he'll tell me the rest tomorrow at the hospital."

"What hospital?" Hugo asked.

She shrugged her shoulders, not wanting to say anything because of what the doc had said to her, and just said, "I have to meet him in Tampa tonight. He has tickets waiting for me at Dulles."

"I'm going with you," Hugo insisted.

"No, you mustn't," Camille vehemently stated, getting up from the table and pulling down on her knee length skirt. She hugged Hugo, walked out, and flagged down a taxi for the airport.

* * *

Camille briskly walked to the terminal exit alongside what appeared to be just another "snowbird" swooping in on the great state of Florida. He was a feeble grey-haired man who seemed barely able to walk. He wore navy blue pants that went down to his ankles and a jacket with sleeves that went halfway up his forearms. He was carrying a purple canvas carryall bag that was much too stuffed to zip, with scarves and hair pieces drooping over its sides. She paid no attention to this old man, however. Once outside, Camille immediately saw the brown Hummer one lane over and climbed inside. The old man followed right behind her in a red taxi.

Camille found the table where the doc was supposed to be. She waited thirty minutes...no doc. These thirty minutes turned into two hours, and still...no doc. Finally Camille called Hugo's cell.

He answered with, "Haven't you figured it out yet?"

Camille replied, "Wait a second. Are you crazy, or am I? What the hell is...." Before she could finish her question, she glanced up and saw Hugo standing at the entrance to the café, a wrinkled pair of blue pants draped over his right forearm and a grey jacket resting on top of his sturdy shoulders. He smiled and motioned to Camille to leave with him.

She jumped up and ran over to him. She grabbed his arm, this time not in a passionate way but in a stern, motherly fashion, and sounded off, using plenty of gestures, as this is what she was used to doing, having grown up in a French-Canadian province. "Let me talk. Don't interrupt me. I want to know everything...and I mean everything...so talk, talk to me, now—now, I said."

Hugo agreed to on the ride back to her home.

When they got to his rental car, Hugo opened its trunk, took the jacket off his back, and placed it inside the purple carryall lying on top of a grey wig and black dress shoes with socks stuffed inside. She questioned him, "What's all that shit for, Hugh?" He slammed the trunk and opened her door, saying nothing.

In silence they motored past Camille's home, only doing about seventy as he heard on the CB that the cops were out in droves. He quickly swerved off the two-lane Gulf Coast road into a public beach parking lot. He parked. They both got out and held hands. He took her behind the pavilion, adjacent to the parking lot, where a more muddy beach area was, and confessed to her that he'd "hit" Doc Martin. "The doc had too much to say for your pretty ears, and he scammed us, too. No one does that to us. I don't want anything to happen to you, precious. You see, I've fallen madly in love with you. I followed you from K Street to Florida disguised as a geeky old man. The stuff you saw in my trunk was my costume. The carryall contains my bag of tricks. It's there when I need it, even when I don't. Its for my survival...it provides my wealth and security. Now I want it to provide for our wealth and security."

Getting more and more scared with each syllable spoken by Hugo, Camille nervously broke into French, without even thinking, and asked, "*Cést que ce? Je ne comprend pas. Je sais que je táime seulmont.*" Hugo loved her more with each foreign word she uttered. He hugged her and hysterically broadcast to her and to the seagulls and the crabs on the beach, "What I want is for you to be my wife. My one wife, forever and ever. I've been waiting all my life for you." He never mentioned that he had had other marriages.

Shocked at hearing this proposal, Camille squatted down on the hard, compacted sand, her head in her hands, and after a silence, which seemed to last a good ten minutes, she looked up at him, into the steel blue eyes a street light was highlighting, and whispered, "Okay."

Hugo thought it now the time and place for her to know the truth about him. He pulled Camille up from her squatting position and held her for a short time. Then he pushed her from his chest, holding her at a distance. He looked deep into her green eyes and said, "I'm in the mob...the Mafia. The Irish version of it."

Her green eyes slowly fell shut and her knees buckled underneath her. Hugo caught her before she fell and revived her by slapping her cheek. When she was totally alert, he clarified to her, "As a mob wife, you'll be part of this world, too, so just keep your mouth shut and we'll be great. You'll have whatever you've ever dreamed of...ya hear?"

"*Trés bien*," Camille replied in an obligatory manner as she held his hand and kissed it.

They drove back to her house, this time continually talking. She changed into a sweat suit and sneakers, made espresso, and the two of them began to plan their wedding.

* * *

The next day they flew to Vegas in a mob-owned jet for a private ceremony.

Chapter Sixteen

The third night back in St. Pete, Camille found the missing piece to the puzzle in her mail box. The wind gusts were blowing and the rain was pouring as she ran toward the house carrying the mail and her large, sturdy black and red-striped umbrella. She had owned this umbrella for over twenty years and had purchased it in an upscale store in Montreal. It had been relatively expensive, but evidently worth it. She and her umbrella had survived numerous rain and snow storms, some quite severe.

She opened the front door, griping three pieces of mail between her lips, and found Hugo sitting on the couch, Heineken in hand, saying, "What ya got there, hon?"

Looking at two return addresses and one postmark, Camille answered in bewilderment, with her nose crinkled, "Looks like two bills and a letter from someone in Santorini, Greece."

Hugo jumped off the couch, wild-eyed, and barked, "Give that damn letter to me."

She jokingly said, "Okay," and put it on top of his head.

He gruffly took it off his head and ripped open the envelope's back, pulling out a note that looked as if it had been written by a child using Crayolas for the first time or a foreigner who didn't know English. The hard to read message, written in black, read:

> Keneth is buried behnd orphanag ner Fenway Park. Ma tyin nevr snubd ya. It was me. The mob maad me do it. You wer so prety and sweete. Pleese forgve me.

Camille cried hysterically, "Get out of my sight, Hugh. All you ever wanted was to play me and my emotions."

Hugo grabbed her and shook her hard until she calmed down and said, "No, I didn't. I fell in love with you, mad love. Francis is playing games with everyone involved. He's like that. I never trusted him. From the minute I laid eyes on him I knew it. You've got to believe me. He's gotten real good at it, too." With a pouty look on his face, he sweetly told her, "We'll get him, though."

After an intense moment of silence, Hugo asked her, "Now, whatta say about being my date tonight?" Camille nodded in approval.

"Now, go clean up and slip into your sexiest outfit, and we'll have the midnight buffet at that quiet, fancy restaurant downtown. You know, the Italian one you like so much. How's about it?" he asked smugly.

"I'm sorry I talked mean to you, Hugh. You know I'd love to be your date tonight," Camille lovingly replied.

"Well then, get off your pretty ass and I'll wait for you outside," Hugo said, his voice trailing off as he walked toward the front door. He reached for the cell he had put on the entry table and walked into the front yard. He shouted that he was going to call the real estate agency to find out about leads on the house.

Staring out her bedroom window in dark silence, Camille watched Hugo ranting animatedly, talking to some other party on his cell. She knew he wasn't calling for the reason he said. No, it was for some other purpose, but she didn't care anymore. She didn't care about the secrets. She loved life with Hugo, and that was that. She didn't want to cause any more waves. She quickly bathed, then put on a low-cut, tight mini-dress with high-heeled clear sandals after painting her toenails and putting on her mascara, blush, and pink lipstick. When she had finished getting ready, she encountered a quiet, more serious Hugo out by the front gate. She asked him what the agents had said.

He was silent, grabbed her hand, walked her to the Cabrio, opened its door, and put her inside, handing her a fifty dollar bill. "Go get a good meal tonight. I have a problem to straighten out," he sternly told her. He shut her door, waved goodbye, and ran inside the house.

* * *

Irwin Stuart sat at his newly-acquired beach bar, feeling the cool Mediterranean dawn breeze. The waitress poured him more strong coffee and served him some powdered sugar cookies. He was sitting in the direction of the infant sunrise, talking loudly to someone on his cell. He waited for three real estate agents to meet him for Bloody Marys before checking out a hot new property visible only from his bar. This property was located off the coast of Santorini and was its own private island, white cement cottage included. It intrigued Irwin when he heard about it, so he had asked his boat hand to call the agency handling the listing to schedule an appointment.

Fifteen minutes later

The three real estate agents were shown to the bar by Nicholas, the boat hand, and introduced to a gracious Irwin. The waitress poured the already mixed strong, spicy tomato juice with the bitter gin that was flown in from Athens. All four men looked at pictures of the island while finishing their morning libations.

After thirty minutes Nicholas yelled, with flailing arms, "Let's go guys." He loaded the motor boat with what appeared to be two rather large first aid cases. After the cases were loaded, he motioned for the four passengers to board and put on life jackets with safety gear because the current was so rough. Once on the small boat, Nicholas hooked the jackets of the four guests onto their respective seats with aluminum straps and metal spring clamps. Next he strapped heavy duty nylon seat belts around their waists, for "added protection."

After a very choppy ten minute boat ride, the five reached the uninhabited isle. Nicholas unlocked Irwin's life jacket and extended his hand out to Irwin, pulling him off the boat and onto dry land. Two of the remaining three were in obvious pain, displaying bloody cuts all over their feminine looking arms, presumably from the sharp, jagged inner aluminum corners of the boat. The two said they must tend to their ailments, using the contents from one of the first aid boxes. Nicholas asked them if they could wait for one second until he got over to the chest. He said he'd be back momentarily to unstrap and unhook them, but he had to first drop off the heavy medicine chest he was carrying at the base of the hill.

Nicholas impatiently said to Irwin, "Come on. We've got to hurry. Got to be back at the bar for the afternoon sunbather crowd."

"Are you sure you've got the right one?" the unscarred passenger nervously asked without thinking.

"Yep," Nicholas grinned, assuring him.

Irwin eyed Nikko wickedly as Nikko pulled out two saturated swabs from the chest and placed one in each of the two agents' hands. The agents just stared at each other in disbelief. Nikko then waved goodbye and started to walk up the sand dune with Irwin. Suddenly Nicholas swung completely around and threw the key in the direction of the motorboat. Laughing hysterically, he shouted to the helpless men, "Let's meet up at the bungalow, soon...okay?" pointing to a small shack up the hill.

The panic-stricken, red-headed, freckle-faced young agent shouted desperately, "This wasn't the plan, Nikko!"

Nicholas answered harshly, smiling from ear to ear, "I know," and continued walking. Irwin smiled at Nick, and nodded.

A couple of seconds later, the three heard a ticking noise coming from the first aid box left on board. The petrified agents screamed and frantically stretched, trying to lift the box and toss it overboard. None could raise it, hardly even grip it, because of its distance from where they were strapped in. It seemed to be weighed down with lead. The redhead screamed in a now detectable Irish accent, "I knew we should have hit you while you were still in the States, but..."

"And I knew," Irwin interrupted passionately, "That you realty boys were owned by the Irish mob and were paid to whack me. Nicholas told me you even paid him to do it," Irwin snickered, as the ticking continued.

Staring a hole through the redhead's fair face, a cocky Irwin stressed, with squinched eyes, "One lesson for you boys to learn is that an Irish mobster can never come between a boss and his right hand man. Nick is as faithful as a puppy to me. He does everything I say and is highly compensated for it."

"I could have got you with one shot at that bank in Lucerne, but they said, 'No, wait,'" The young man screamed out.

"Another lesson for you boys to learn is, never look in the *rear view mirror*," Irwin sarcastically broke-in, knowing he possessed the winning hand. "It could provide for your demise."

"You cocksuck—." Before the young Irishman could finish his comments of angst, a firey explosion sounded and engulfed the motorboat with flames, sending body and boat parts flying throughout the mid-morning sky.

'Irwin' and Nicholas trudged to the other side of the isle, arm-in-arm, and embarked on their yacht. Their planned deed was now done and over.

* * *

One week later on the Italian island of Sardenia at a beach bar

"Hey, girls. Come on over here let me buy you a drink and tell you a story. Sit down. Daiquiris are on the way. My name is Tex, and I'm from Texas," he chuckled, stroking his moustache. He continued the charade, using his new-found southern accent, "I come from generations of oil in West Texas. I'm rich, and I'm very successful," he boasted, as he flung his long, dark, wavy locks of hair over his shoulder.

Nikko stood by and watched Irwin break into his new personae, laughing under his breath all the while as he listened to the rehearsed scrip, thinking of the necessities he had learned from Irwin over the past few months, especially regarding role-playing. He also had become aware, quite frequently, of how Francis liked both genders, and all ages. He moaned and groaned in disgust as he turned his head away from the crowd, "Onli won moore nite."

When the bar emptied at nightfall, he and Francis walked back to their bungalow. Nikko had seen and heard hundreds of Irwin's characters, but, "This portrayal was by far the best," he told Francis, laughing all the while. He was sure that Tex would have become Francis's new identity, but now it was too late...'cause now the gig was up and now the time was right.

Francis walked into their room through the sliding glass door and said, "I'm gonna hit the sack. Join me when you can."

Nikko nodded and opened up his suitcase on the patio and took out a bottle of codeine and a bottle of brandy. He shook out seven six-hundred milligram pills and poured a large amount of brandy in a snifter.

Thirty minutes later, Nicholas nudged and awakened Francis by saying, "Cume on. Waak up. I jus wanna to hve a nitecap wit ya," to which Francis readily agreed. When Francis was sufficiently hammered and passed out, Nikko put him on the couch and stuffed the seven codeines down his numb throat.

Nikko walked from the room onto the beach and found a strong, thick rope, which he wrapped around a heavy piece of driftwood he found lying on top of the sand. He, artistically, wrote in the sand, with his new-found writing utensil, "Nicholas Pporkas, bote hand, alias Nathan Starkey...." He stopped and maniacally belted out a deep chuckle from his belly. When he did this, he glanced in and saw Francis snoring through the open door. He loved knowing Francis was so alive and so peaceful now and, in only a few minutes, would be dead and gone from civilization, all because of him. Nicholas felt powerful now, for the first time in his life. Everything was going well for him, both personally and professionally. He had become a clone of Francis. No longer was he a struggling non-entity on this planet. He knew he would become a billionaire in less than ten years, with all the right moves, strategies, and deceit. He had learned from an expert. "Nicholas Sporkas, bote hand, alias Nathan Starkey....." He continued with his dribble in the sand, "Unemployd California beach bum, wil inhearit evrythin...in won splt secnd. Th' five hundrid tuenti-five fukin' millon, now licuid, that th' mob, an Francis, haad schemd so longe and haard to get, now belons ta mi...all ta mi...an ugli graade schewl drawpout frum Mykonos. I outsmartd the wirld. An th' saad parte is...it was eezy!"

* * *

Camille's old Florida cell phone rang three consecutive times, almost off the hook. It would ring, then stop, then ring again. Alone in the estate, as Hugo had gone to Maine for a business negotiation trip, she didn't want to be bothered, but she hesitantly answered her cell. She didn't know who would be calling her at this number after eight at night. Her husband and mother only called on the home phone or Camille's new Boston-based cellular number. She looked at the displayed number, lit up in the middle of the receiver, before saying anything. She screamed. The number on caller identification was Kenneth's ranch in Bradenton.

Frightened, she answered, "What?"

A voice merrily sounded out, "Wanna meet me at Fresco's, where the prices are right, and the martinis are sizzlin', Zahz? Can't wait, 'cause I love you so."

Her mistreated heart finally gave out on her. She sank down into the carpet and withered away, not breathing at all. Since she had met Kenneth at the pier that day, life had become much too rough for her. She had become frail and thin.

Her newlywed husband then walked through the front door and went into the bedroom, where he saw his bride lying on the wood floor. "Good. Dead as a doornail. Now I don't have to do it!," he said hastily, knowing he'd soon collect the five million dollar life insurance policy he had just taken out on Camille and that he would be the one to collect all her house proceeds, since she had put him on a quick claim deed a few days prior.

* * *

Hugo boarded the jet to Athens, with his "bag of disguises." When he arrived in Greece, he was met in a vacant back corner of the arrival terminal by a timid Nicholas, who handed him a large, heavy duffel bag.

Hugo then forced the concealed silencer into Nikko's stomach and fired it. Nikko hit the tiled floor and his gun fell out of his limp hand.

Hugo opened Nikko's duffel, saw the money stuffed inside, zipped it back up, and kept on walking, with one bag in each hand toward the taxi, toward freedom, smiling and laughing all the way. "Oh, how fate wheels and deals," he victoriously said to himself, holding his brand new Mazzarati keys in hand, along with keys to his new ten thousand square foot villa, both he had bought while living in St. Petersburg and which were waiting for him up the road.

Will I ever know true happiness? he thought while becoming "Nikko" in the backseat for close to an hour. His eyes watered as a vision of Camille briefly passed through his mind. When the taxi came to an abrupt halt, however, his tears quickly dried up. The master of disguises had transformed his frowning face into a face with a lengthy smile stretched across it. He couldn't believe his eyes as he stared at his elaborate estate, equipped with his favorite orange-haired playmate, Sophie, from Corsica, sitting inside the Mazzarati.

Hugo paid the taxi driver, who opened the back door for him to get out, and Hugo said "Thanks."

The driver only stared at him, then he threw Hugo's money on the ground and pulled out a short revolver, staring at the Irishman's face in disgust. He screamed to Hugo, "This one's for my boy, Nikko. You're not him, never will be. This party's gonna end now." The driver then spit on Hugo, fired bullets, and drove through the electric gates, using his sensor pad, and into the estate, which was bought by Hugo, a.k.a. Nikko.

An Irish real estate agent Francis had known and worked with in the past had called Nikko three days before and informed him that the keys to his estate were left underneath the gargantuous front doormat at the mansion. Nikko and his father were more than surprised and decided to play the scenario out to see what would happen next in the plot. Well, they did, and they both found Hugo to be the evil force in the story.

Nikko had first talked to Hugo on the telephone when Hugo called Francis from St. Petersburg late one night, shouting at him wildly and threatening him. Only on one other occasion did they speak. This was when Nicholas and Hugo agreed to be partners in another big money "characterization" crime, of course after Francis' death. To start off their partnership on the right foot, Hugo requested that Nicholas meet him that morning in the Athen's airport to give him a portion of this last take. Nikko was carrying only a small amount of Irwin's stashed cash in a duffel, supposed to be Hugo's share of the take. Nicholas, and his father, who was waiting in the taxi outside the exit, had planned to shoot Hugo with their short revolver as soon as he plopped down in the back seat. Hugo, however, was too experienced to let this happen. He knew not to trust anyone, and besides, he wanted all of the take, not only a small portion. He knew he had to kill...first.

* * *

The taxi driver lived at the estate now. Nikko's father was sole heir, being Nikko's only living relative. Bullets filled the evening sky. This high stakes masquerade was over. Hugo was lying face down in the bloody grass, silencer by his side. "What a pity...but it was self-defense," the new rich mogul sarcastically said to his playmate. He phoned for the police.

Then he pulled out a bottle from the trunk and poured a sparkling glass of Prosecco.